An Eerie Welcome
to St. Anne Manor

The cab squealed to a stop in the driveway, and Cary paid her fare and got out. As it drove away she hurried up the steps to the front door. Before she could knock, however, the door swung open from her on creaking hinges. A wraithlike figure stood in the inner darkness. Despite the sunken eyes, straggling hair, and defeated posture, Cary recognized her friend.

"Charon!" Overcoming her horror at the dramatic change in her friend's appearance, Cary squealed greeting and flung her arms around the girl. "Oh, Charon, it's so good to see you again!"

"Oh, Cary, I'm so glad you came! I've missed you all these years." Charon kissed Cary's cheek, then drew away. Tears of joy streamed down her cheeks.

"Oh, me too!" Cary clasped Charon's hands and squeezed them. "But what's wrong? Your letter scared me. Please tell me it's nothing—that my overactive imagination ran amok and actually you're doing fine. What happened anyway?"

Charon smiled sadly as she brushed a lank strand of beige hair from her face. "What indeed?" She murmured scarcely above a whisper. "Someone's trying to kill me that's what."

Deadly Friendship

Candice Arkham

AVON
PUBLISHERS OF BARD, CAMELOT, DISCUS, EQUINOX AND FLARE BOOKS

DEADLY FRIENDSHIP is an original publication of Avon Books. This work has never before appeared in any form.

AVON BOOKS
A division of
The Hearst Corporation
959 Eighth Avenue
New York, New York 10019

First Avon Printing, October, 1973.

Printed in the U.S.A.

Prologue

Old Gumbo Jack's smiling-eyed Tina, a happy child of five, had been the first to disappear. She had been taught never to wander past the high ground on which their swamp cabin faced the gloomy marsh, yet now she was gone.

Out beyond was the bayou, a place hostile to little girls. In its muddied waters, alligators floated with only cold eyes exposed to watch for prey, while glittering snakes slithered in winding paths along the surface. Serpents—some poisonous like the cottonmouth, and some not so deadly, thrived in the bayou's foul smelling mud.

Worst of all, in Gumbo Jack's eyes, was the quicksand. Treacherous. An innocent looking patch of damp land, only it would suck you down and bury you alive before anyone had even missed you. He knew, because it had almost happened to him once. Perhaps, he thought, it had been the quicksand that had claimed his Tina. Jack shuddered at that most horrifying possibility.

He had last seen his girl two mornings ago. Her chubby hand had been raised to wave goodby as he paddled his pirogue out to the day's work of finding food. When he had returned that evening, the cabin's oppressive silence had filled him with the certainty that something had gone wrong. Opening the door, he had found Rex, the child's collie, dead with his throat torn out. The little girl herself was gone.

One week later, a second disappearance took place in the nearby village of Fleur-de-Lis, when the infant son of

Jean and Marie Lalique was stolen from his bed. Following the baby, three more children were gone—young ones, but old enough to know better than to wander the swamp alone.

Whispers spread from ear to ear, each mouth muttering the same word. It was one so heavy with the legacy of terror that even strong men crossed themselves when they uttered it. Loup-garou, the half-forgotten myth revived in all its primal horror.

Eyes turned once more down the mud road to fix with hatred upon St. Anne Manor. A brooding, white pillared mansion built years before the Civil War, this rotting, tumble-down structure, though originally set upon high ground, had sunk into its gloomy marshland estate by the weight of time. It stood silent, surrounded by an oppressive aura of evil.

Madame Dapogny, a withered hag of unnumbered years, remembered tales of the manor's early days—of slaves tortured and killed; but it had all happened before she was born, or so she said.

Other old villagers, decades younger than Madame Dapogny, had been told the tale as children of how Louis Parveau, descendant of the original master, had stabbed his beautiful young wife Sophie in a fit of drunken jealousy.

Within their own lives, but many years ago, rumors of unspeakable orgies and obscene rites had come out of the place. During times when weird lights flickered behind St. Anne Manor's dirty windows, young women had disappeared—sometimes to be found later, dead in the swamp with throats ripped open and veins bled dry.

Within the past five months, wanderers and hunters who had passed the old mansion late at night reported that there were lights again in some of the windows. St. Anne Manor's deserted rooms had returned to life, and now the children were being taken, one by one. As more disappeared, the people's mood became like kindling wood—ready to ignite at the smallest spark.

Chapter One

Cary Matthews peered eagerly out of the old taxicab's
open side window as the silent bayou sped by and searched
for any signs that they were soon to arrive at St. Anne
Manor.

The motor droned steadily, its well-oiled purr vibrating
against Cary's back as she leaned into the soft vinyl of the
door. She stared out at the listless trees whose gnarled
roots took nourishment from the swamp mud. Draped
from their languid branches, tendrils of parasitic moss hung
slack in the muggy heat.

Cary sighed wearily as she wiped the back of one arm
across her sweating forehead. Squirming, she shifted her
weight to another part of the seat, for perspiration soaking
through her skirt made it sticky when she stayed on one
spot too long. It was the end of October and the weather
had grown unseasonably warm. Indian summer, they would
have called it back in Ohio, from where she had just come.
Down here in Louisiana Cary didn't know what they called
this fall heat.

Tingling numbness in Cary's right foot told her it had
gone to sleep. "Drat!" she muttered, and as she kicked to
force some circulation back into her toes, glanced at her
hands. With surprise she noticed that both were clenched
into tight fists. Opening them flat, Cary frowned, bewildered, knowing that she made fists only when nervous. But
what had she to be nervous about? Here she was, on her
way to see Charon, her close friend and former college
roommate, and instead of feeling happy at the prospect of

7

renewing old gossip and memories, Cary felt jumpy, on edge. But why?

She reached into her purse and pulled out the now wrinkled letter that had summoned her to St. Anne Manor. Scanning its terse lines, she tried to read meaning into its message.

Dear Cary,
Please come down as soon as possible. I need you here. You can take a bus from the N.O. International Airport to Lafayette and a cab from there to here, and I'll be more than happy to repay your costs. Wire your reply. If needed, I'll wire you plane fare, but please, oh please, come!

Yours,
Charon

From the muted plea of those words, as well as the way Charon's usually crisp handwriting had altered into a hasty sprawl, Cary had sensed fear, even panic behind the written message. That, more than anything else, worried her. Charon had always been the calm, clear-eyed one. At the exclusive women's college they had both attended—Cary on a scholarship and Charon from the interest on an inheritance held in trust—Charon had always been coolly sensible. She had been the first to scoff at astrology, tarot, and all the other fashionable superstitions. Even in politics she had been able to see both sides of any issue. What had happened in the past five years to change her—to frighten her so? Cary shuddered with unexplainable dread. Shaking her head to rid herself of the feeling, she jammed the message back into her purse with suddenly trembling hands. No use thinking about it until she knew all the facts, she reflected.

"When will we get there?" she asked. "I mean, you're sure we're not lost?"

Glancing into the rear view mirror, Cary noticed the driver raise his eyebrows. He was a thick man, stolid and rounded. In a gray cabby uniform with his hunched shoulders and broad sunburned neck jutting forward, he reminded Cary of a water-smoothed boulder. He paused before answering.

"The map says it's five miles down the road past Fleur-de-Lis," he drawled, "an' we ain't hit Fleur-de-Lis yet."

"Can we stop awhile then? My foot's going to sleep and I'd like to walk around a minute or two."

"Almost to Fleur-de-Lis now," he said, shrugging. "Have to stop for gas anyhow. Be jest a few minutes."

Cary's hand slid across the seat to pick at a wisp of gray stuffing that escaped from a hole worn into its scratched, cigarette-burned surface. With a sigh, she wondered if she might not have made a mistake in coming. But when she remembered The Anthill, her name for the highrise insurance conglomerate where she had been bored and miserable in a job she hated, Cary knew better. No, there was nothing to keep her in Cleveland, especially after learning the truth about Bob.

Tears bleared her eyes as Cary remembered his face, those twinkling gray eyes, gazing so honestly into hers as he told her lie after lie. She had believed him. It was only later that she found out about his wife and the two yellow-haired little girls they had adopted. One thing about Bob though, she reflected, he had taught her never to take things at face value.

Clenching teeth in hurt and anger, Cary turned to stare again at the passing bayou. The sun, casting mottled shadows through the lush canopy of overhead branches, shown golden yellow as it sank below view behind tangled vegetation. She sighed again. Unable to hide her growing discomfort, Cary wondered if nightfall brought relief from the sweltering heat.

Uninhabited swamp began to give way to a settlement of scattered shacks. These, removed from being cabins only by virtue of once painted walls and front porches no longer able to support the weight of their own roofs, mingled side by side with kidney-shaped trailers of old-fashioned design. Set upon blocks instead of wheels, orange-brown rust covered their once silver sides, while flies swarmed over dog piles randomly scattered on unplanted dirt yards.

When they reached a green and white bungalow with two gas pumps out front, her driver pulled in beside the closest. A swarthy youth ran out from the freshly painted front entrance. Reaching the cab, he greeted its inhabitants.

"Good afternoon, may I help you?" His accent, typically

9

Cajun, sounded peculiar to Cary's ears—not Southern, but not quite French either. As Cary threw open her door and stumbled out, he smiled at her. "You going far?" he asked, sticking the gas hose into the cab's trunk.

"No, just down the road." Cary stretched, then sighed in relief. "A place called St. Anne Manor. Perhaps you've heard of it?"

The smile faded from the youth's face. His broad low forehead furrowed into a scowl as he shook his head. "Why're you going there?" Cary turned to him, surprised at the hint of horror she saw in his suddenly glazed eyes.

"I'm going because I've been invited." Her voice sounded sharp, even rude as she tried to suppress a sudden spasm of anxiety.

"Don't go, Miss," he said. His black eyes fixed on hers. "Turn back."

At his words, the old nervous edginess had rushed back upon Cary, its return exasperating her. "I'll go wherever I please," she said, stamping back into the car. As Cary slammed the door, she glanced back, shocked to see the young Cajun crossing himself.

"Sure you still want to, lady?" The driver turned to stare questioningly at her troubled face. "I heard what the boy said."

"Yes, I still want to go there." Cary fought to keep a tremor out of her voice, but failed. "Now please let's get going!" The driver started the motor and lurched forward, remaining silent as he drove the final few miles to St. Anne Manor.

The youth's reaction worried her. What was going on at St. Anne Manor to create such fear among the nearby villagers? The boy had actually tried to scare her off. He failed only because Cary wasn't the kind of person to let a friend down when she was needed. As much as she wanted to turn back, she couldn't abandon Charon. After all, Charon hadn't turned away when Cary needed help. Her scholarship had run out during her senior year. If it hadn't been for Charon, generously coming to her aid with enough money to supplement savings from the part-time job she had taken, Cary might never have graduated. Even though she had long since paid back the money itself, Cary nevertheless felt deeply indebted to Charon for the trust

10

and kindness she had shown when Cary needed it most. For that reason, no matter what was going on at St. Anne Manor, Cary had to see it through.

"Well, here it is." The driver grunted doubtfully as he turned onto a rutted driveway leading to the rambling brick mansion. The place reminded Cary of all the Civil War movies she had ever seen, and she itched to capture it with brushes and canvas.

Beneath the peeling white paint, the walls beneath were pocked and worn. Extending out around the lower story was a broad porch, its tiled roof supported by tall, white columns. On the second story, French windows opened onto lacy wrought-iron balconies painted white to match the house. Tall willows and cypresses, growing on the grounds in thick profusion, cast long shadows. These lent the mansion an overwhelming atmosphere of darkness and gloom. The cab squealed to a stop in the driveway, and Cary paid her fare and got out.

As it drove away, she hurried up the steps to the front door. Before she could knock, however, the door swung away from her on creaking hinges. A wraithlike figure stood in the inner darkness. Despite the sunken eyes, straggling hair and defeated posture, Cary recognized her friend.

"Charon!" Overcoming her horror at the dramatic change in Charon's appearance, Cary squealed greeting and flung her arms around the girl. "Oh, Charon, it's so good to see you again!"

"Oh, Cary, I'm so glad you came! I've missed you all these years." Charon kissed Cary's cheek, then drew away. Tears of joy streamed down her cheeks.

"Oh, me too!" Cary clasped Charon's hands and squeezed them. "But what's wrong? Your letter scared me. Please tell me it's nothing—that my overactive imagination ran amok and actually you're doing fine." But as she smiled at her friend, Cary found herself shocked that the pallid, pathetic creature standing in front of her was the same blond, efficient girl she had known in college. "What happened anyway?" She asked the question lightly, carefully keeping the horror out of her voice.

Charon smiled sadly as she brushed a lank strand of beige hair from her face. "What indeed?" She murmured scarcely above a whisper. "Someone's trying to kill me, that's what." As Charon answered, her voice changed to an almost casual, conversational tone. Hearing those words, Cary felt a sudden chill. Had Charon gone mad? "Little accidents," continued the girl, "that could have been fatal but weren't. Too many."

Cary followed her into the hallway's chill gloom. Faded wallpaper dissolved into dusty shadows that reached out from the corners and unknown rooms beyond. Before her eyes had a chance to discern the cracks that ran across the papered plaster, or the thick, complex spider webbing in the corners where ceiling met wall, Charon motioned toward an ornate, winding stairway.

"I've prepared your room." Her once clear voice was altered by a quality of breathlessness Cary hadn't noticed before. "I'll take you there now, before the others get back."

Cary followed Charon up a narrowly twisting flight of steps. She let her fingers slide pensively over the dull, ornately carved hardwood bannister, trying to imagine the time when that untended walnut must have been polished to a glistening sheen. She thought of the glittering balls that might have been held there once—of the belles whose lashes fluttered behind lace fans, courted by dandies who later marched away—destined to die in the Civil War. Perhaps the place is haunted, she thought with grim relish.

At the top, Charon whirled, staring down at Cary with fear stricken eyes. "Oh I'm so glad you've come," she cried. "I've felt so alone here, so afraid ever since—"

Suddenly Charon tottered, pressing a hand against her forehead, then groaned. Cary charged up the steps between them, reaching out to seize her faltering friend as she collapsed unconscious into Cary's arms.

Chapter Two

Cary sat beside Charon, exhausted from the effort it had taken to drag her to the nearest bed. As her mind whirled with a rush of unanswered questions, she waited patiently for Charon's return to consciousness. At last the girl's pale lashes fluttered open and Cary leaned forward eagerly.

"Charon?" Her half-whispered greeting urged her friend to respond.

After a few seconds, Charon's glazed blue eyes focused and a weak smile played upon her lips.

"Thank you," she whispered. Her frail hand groped for Cary's sturdy fingers and held them in a weak grip. Her large eyes fixed pleadingly on Cary's. "Help me!" Charon's voice faltered.

"What is it? I can't until I know what's wrong." Cary stared at her in alarm.

"That's just it." Charon sighed. "I don't really know myself." Her brows pinched together into a frown. "But something's going on. Everybody acts the same outwardly, but inwardly—well, that's different." Charon shuddered and looked away. "There are evil forces at work in this house, Cary, and I'm too weak to fight them by myself, or even to understand them."

Trying to pretend an eagerness she didn't feel, Cary leaned forward. "Charon, you've got to get away from here. This morbid house—it's bad for you. It's your isolation that's made you ill. I'm going out to Los Angeles soon. Come with me! We can find jobs and share an apartment. It'll do you good!"

13

Charon smiled bitterly. "It's no use. I can't really explain it so that you'd understand, but I can't leave this place—not yet. Sometimes I feel that I'll never leave. That it won't let me go."

"Nonsense!" Cary spoke sharply, reversing the roles both young women had taken in college. Somehow she had to shake her friend out of this strange morbidity.

"Even so, I can't leave any more than the others can. They feel it too. I know they do."

"Who are the others? Friends? Relatives?" Cary felt curious. She had always thought Charon was completely alone in the world, an orphan with only the National Bank and Trust of New Orleans to protect her.

"There's Aunt Marie, who really isn't my aunt, of course. She's staying here along with her half sister, whom I've always called Aunt Janette. Actually they're both old and trusted servants who've lived here since before I was born. Flora is the live-in housekeeper, and then there's Jerico."

"Charon!"

A voice, breaking from behind into their conversation, startled Cary. The tones were firm but elderly, and as Cary whirled she saw the woman who had uttered them. "Dinner is to be served on the sunporch."

She was a tall person who held herself stiffly erect. Though her face was gaunt and wrinkled, it held hint of former beauty in its fine boned structure. The clear black eyes were focused levelly into Cary's own, betraying none of the woman's inner feelings. Her gray hair, pulled severely back, was held in place by tortoise-shell combs. From her bony shoulders hung a simple black dress. She wore a tiny silver cross suspended from a chain around her neck.

"Oh, Aunt Marie." Charon's voice came out as a weak murmur. "This is Cary. Cary Matthews. Do you remember I told you she might be coming down to visit me?"

"Yes, I remember," replied the old woman. She turned to Cary, studying her severely. "Has Miss Charon shown you to your room yet?"

"N–no." Awed by the woman's cold civility, she stammered like a shy schoolchild. "You see, Charon fell ill, and—"

"I quite understand." Marie took the situation firmly

14

under control. "You may follow me, please. She'll be safe enough now."

Cary walked behind Marie along the dim hallway, not daring to break the old woman's grim silence. When Marie reached a closed door at the far end, she turned its knob. As the door swung open, she turned to Cary and stared intently.

"Charon has a very vivid imagination." Her voice sounded harsh and strained. "I think you shouldn't have come."

Cary drew in her breath sharply. "I came because Charon sent a letter asking me here." Unspoken questions rushed to her mind. Charon had never seemed morbidly imaginative before, yet today she had almost frightened Cary with her talk of evil forces and death. It wasn't like her. But what if Charon hadn't changed? What if wickedness really did exist in this house? If so, what could Cary, a twenty-six-year-old insurance underwriter from Cleveland, do about it? Suddenly she felt very helpless.

Marie frowned, then cleared her throat to recapture Cary's attention. "I hope you find your room comfortable." The old woman forced an icy smile as she nodded toward the chamber.

"Oh, I'm sure I shall!" cried Cary in delight as she saw it. Wallpaper of a delicate gray, black and silver fleur-de-lis pattern covered the walls. In a smaller room this might have been too dark, but here, with the huge windows leading out onto a flower-planted balcony, the design and colors were perfect. Shiny white woodwork contrasted with the walls, as did the cotton eyelet canopy and quilt on the mahogany four-poster bed. The room also had a roll-top desk and dresser, both mahogany like the bed, as well as a comfortable looking easy chair. "It's beautiful!" She murmured in honest appreciation. "That balcony—is it functional? I mean, can I sit out there if I please?"

"You can if you wish, though you might find the mosquitoes and flies too voracious for you. The swamp spawns them." The old woman turned to leave, then fixed her eyes on Cary with piercing stare. "About Charon. You mustn't take what she says too seriously. She's been ill with brain fever and still suffers from morbid fancies. Do you understand?"

15

Cary sighed in relief, then nodded as she silently watched the old woman back away. Brain fever! That was an explanation Cary's rational mind could easily grasp. A serious but mundane physical ailment had developed from Charon's unhealthy swamp surroundings leaving her mind temporarily weakened, vulnerable to suggestion. "Poor Charon!" Cary shook her head in pity. Once alone in her room, she closed the door and began to unpack.

As she reached into the bottom desk drawer to put away her stationery, Cary accidentally touched a spring latch. To her surprise, a false bottom popped open. Curious, she reached into the darkness below and groped for whatever might be hidden there. Instead of finding a stash of worthless and forgotten confederate money or an heirloom jewel, Cary's fingers touched by what its shape could only be a book. She pulled it out and to her surprise saw that the thin, sour smelling little volume was bound in maroon leather. The word 'Lycaon', tooled in gold Gothic lettering across the front and binding, was, Cary presumed, the title. Opening it gingerly, she studied its contents, printed on brittle, yellowed parchment.

Cary wished she had been a better student when she studied Latin in school, because the words she recognized from the little tome's archaic script tantalized her mightily. She was able to translate the Latin words for *death, blood, wolf* and *night,* and those few indicated highly entertaining reading.

Just then, a knocking on her closed door startled Cary. Without understanding why, she furtively slipped the little book back into that bottom drawer, closed it, then turned. "Come in." Her voice suddenly quavered in guilty embarrassment.

The door opened slowly. Standing in the hall, a scrawny, big bellied woman stared at Cary with unabashed curiosity. Her gray hair, twisted into tortuous pincurls held fast by criss-crossed bobbypins, was pulled off a high, but not too particularly intelligent forehead. Thin brows, plucked almost to nonexistence, raised high in surprise under the woman's rather vapid brown eyes. A faded, zipperfront house dress covered her slack body, while scuffed black wedgies had been slipped over the white anklets on her feet.

16

"Yes, what is it?" Cary fought to keep the impatient edge out of her voice. She was annoyed at the interruption, but felt obligated to be nice. Without really knowing why, Cary sensed she didn't like this woman.

"I'm Flora." She spoke with a coy grin. "Miss Marie told me t'tell that dinner's ready." The woman's harshly unpleasant drawl contrasted with her almost childish manner of speaking.

"Thank you, Flora," replied Cary primly. "I'll be down in just a minute." Flora turned and clunked heavily down the hall—leaving behind the distinct odor of whiskey.

"My God," muttered Cary, "the woman sounds like she's wearing clogs!" Chuckling rather uncharitably at Flora's expense, she smoothed her hair before joining the others at dinner.

Chapter Three

Dinner that night, which consisted of a strangely spiced gumbo, was a strained affair. Cary felt uncomfortably out of place sharing a meal with strangers, yet realized that she must use the opportunity to assess her fellow inhabitants of St. Anne Manor. Although Charon, as proper mistress, took her place at the head of the table, it was Marie, sitting at the foot, who guided the conversation by her taciturn remarks and stony silences.

Janette, Marie's younger half sister, sat on Charon's right. She was a small, plump woman of about sixty. Like Marie, Janette's wrinkled complexion tended toward a deep tan hue. Her slightly almond-shaped eyes were dark and alert, and her wavy, once black hair had turned almost pure gray. She rolled it into a wisping untidy bun fastened at the nape of her neck. Her face was pleasantly round, and her thick features were noteworthy for the deep dimples that appeared in her cheeks and chin whenever she smiled. She studied Cary shyly from under genteelly lowered eyelids, hoping perhaps, that the young visitor wouldn't notice.

"Have you lived here all your life, Janette?" Although Cary wasn't deeply interested in the plump spinster's personal history, she sensed it might be useful to have as many people on her side as possible. Why she felt that way Cary didn't understand, but an instinctive warning had flashed in her mind the minute she had set foot on the St. Anne estate.

"Ever since I was a little girl." As Janette replied in her

soft, mild voice, she smiled shyly at Cary. "I'm afraid I haven't traveled much. This has always been my home." She spoke the sentence with weird emphasis, then shrugged. "But then in my day, young ladies were more protected. I once saw New Orleans though."

"How long do you plan to stay with us, Cary?" Marie's cold yet polite question cut into her half sister's narrative, leaving Cary with a strangely unwelcome feeling. What you're asking, mused the practical young woman cynically, is how much longer do you have to put up with me? But Cary wasn't easily intimidated. "Oh, I don't know," she replied breezily. "I suppose as long as Charon wants me to stay." Cary's eyes flitted questioningly to the figure of her friend who had slumped at the head of the table. Charon responded by sitting straighter. She turned to the woman she called her aunt.

"I want her to stay. I want her here. After all," she added, almost defiantly, "I'm mistress of St. Anne Manor and I have the right—"

"Of course you do," murmured Marie soothingly. It seemed to Cary almost as if pacifying Charon was Marie's way of avoiding an unpleasant and revealing scene. Cary's mind lingered upon her own choice of the unspoken word 'revealing'. What was there to hide? Cary, a great believer in the power of her subconscious, wondered if perhaps it might be trying to tell her something.

To Marie's left sat a brooding youth of sixteen—Marie's orphaned grandnephew Jerico. Loose and lanky as boys that age often are, he had a shock of thick black unmanageable hair. Although short by modern standards, it hung uncombed and seemed longer than it actually was. He had set his face into a sour and surly scowl. Despite his skin, which had broken out in mild acne, Jerico's facial bone structure was clearly fine and remarkably similar to Marie's. His intense almond-shaped eyes and the intelligent set of his mouth showed promise of a handsome man emerging. Cary found herself scrutinizing the boy, fascinated with what she saw under the layers of dirt, acne and sullenness.

"Do you still go to school?" she asked. It turned out to be a bad question, but Cary really didn't know enough about him to realize that.

19

Jerico stared at her scornfully, almost angrily. "Hasn't my dear aunt told you already?" His biting sarcasm made Cary flinch. "My late, unlamented school, the Le Beau Military Academy for Boys in Baton Rouge, has just thrown me out for being a hopeless incorrigible, a misfit, and a corrupting influence on my fellow students. Although how one can be both a misfit and a corrupting influence seems to be a mystery," he added bitterly. "After all, no one associates enough with a misfit to become corrupted—"

"Jerico, that will do!" Marie spoke sternly, glaring at him angrily as she overwhelmed the youth with the icy tones of absolute authority. "I don't care to discuss either your failings or the school's while we're eating dinner."

Jerico immediately fell silent, while Cary bit her lip in embarrassment. She felt an almost overwhelming rush of pity for the boy.

"You must tell me about your job," continued Marie in an attempt to gloss over the preceding scene. "Insurance must be so interesting."

"I'm afraid it's nothing of the sort," replied Cary. "Oh, I imagine insurance investigating can be absorbing if you can get into it, but what I was doing was basically clerical. I'm afraid it was hideously boring."

"Are you on vacation?" Marie seemed eager to know of Cary's remaining links with Cleveland.

"No, I quit."

"Oh." Marie's flat tone of voice revealed disappointment.

"Tell me about Cleveland," urged Jerico eagerly. "It's probably much better than any city down here."

Cary smiled faintly. It seemed to be a universal trait of human nature to want what you didn't have. "The climate is different," she replied, "and the setting. The important thing is to be doing what you want to with your life though. If you're not, then one place is as bad as another." She hadn't meant to come off sounding pompous, but those were her true feelings after having worked in three different cities at jobs she basically hated.

"What do you want to do with your life?" asked Marie.

"Painting," replied Cary suddenly. "I've always been more interested in art than anything else. But I'm not commercial enough, so I work at other jobs to pay the rent." She forced a smile. "Perhaps it's just as well. I

20

doubt the world really needs the kind of stuff I do. Anyway, I'm out of practice."

"Your art was always so mystical," murmured Charon. "I remember one landscape you did for an art class—a scene in the Catskills I think it was. It seemed as if a soul were caught in that one old oak tree."

"That's not what you said then," replied Cary drily. "You accused me of being maudlin and melodramatic."

Just then Flora came shuffling in from the kitchen, still dressed in the same dirty shift, anklets and wedgies. Cary wondered idly if the woman ever took her hair out of pin curls.

"Dessert's ready!" She mumbled, slurring her speech slightly. "Should I bring it in?"

"Yes, Flora," replied Marie. "But you could clear the table first."

While Flora scuffled around, clanging dishes and silver, no one spoke. During this period, Cary digested what she had learned of St. Anne Manor's inmates. Surely none of them could have inspired the ghastly warning made by that young Cajun gas station attendant. Eccentric all, but certainly harmless enough, even Jerico. The worst Cary could imagine of him might be stealing cars, and that was hardly enough to paralyze a sturdy villager with fear. Cary wondered if there might be someone she hadn't yet met.

Chapter Four

Cary faced her friend later that same night. Standing in Charon's bedroom, she gazed steadily into the girl's eyes. "Exactly what's going on here, anyway?"

"What do you mean?" Charon's eyelids flickered guiltily and Cary sensed that her friend was hiding something from her.

"On my way here, we stopped in Fleur-de-Lis for gas. The boy at the gas station warned me against coming here. I want to know why. What is it about St. Anne Manor that frightens those people so?"

Charon averted her eyes. "I don't know. I really don't. Those backwoods Cajuns are so superstitious—"

Cary stared in silent exasperation at Charon. It was unlike her to be so strangely defensive. Biting her lip uncertainly, she hesitated to press more heavily for the truth, then finally decided to let things stand for now. She'd pretend to accept Charon's words at face value even though Cary sensed in them a lie. Most of all, it was her own weariness, overwhelming her suddenly after a day of active travel that prompted Cary's response. "Well, perhaps you're right." She shrugged. "People who live off from civilization are often superstitious." She noticed, as she spoke, Charon's eyes brightening in relief. She turned to leave.

"Cary?" Charon's voice wavered pleadingly. "You're-you're not a heavy sleeper are you? I mean, you don't take pills to make you drowsy or anything, do you?"

"No." Startled by the question, Cary gave her friend a puzzled frown. "Why?"

"Oh, nothing really." Charon forced a nervous laugh and a light tone. "I just wondered if you had picked up any bad habits since college. Well, good night!" As she settled into her pillow, she seemed to withdraw totally from any further communication.

Cary walked back to her own room, located next to Charon's on the left side of the hall's spiral staircase and pondered her friend's strange reactions to the question of the villagers' fear of St. Anne Manor. Even stranger was the girl's own peculiar interrogation. Why would Charon be so interested in whether or not Cary was a heavy sleeper or took drugs? Cary knew that people with mental problems often imagined that others shared the same weakness. She wondered if the young heiress herself could be on drugs. Perhaps the story about brain fever had been used merely to cover up what the stern old woman considered a disgraceful addiction. And in Charon's final farewell of the evening, Cary had sensed the undercurrents of a dismissal. She sighed, wishing she could get to the bottom of things.

In the privacy of her room, Cary puttered around a little, then settled down in bed with one of the novels she had brought down with her from Cleveland. The *Lycaon* tome, she had decided, would have to wait until she was less tired and her head was clearer. She walked over to the desk, sprang the secret latch and groped in the darkness just to make sure the thing was safely where it belonged. Then she changed into her nightgown.

After reading for about an hour, an overwhelming desire to sleep caught up with her, so Cary turned out the light.

Her slumbers that night were exceptionally sound, untroubled by outside noises or even dreams. She awakened early. Opening her eyes to the bright sunlight that streamed through the freshly polished window glass, she smiled in contentment. The fears of yesterday were temporarily forgotten. Cary decided, as she luxuriated in the pretty surroundings and crisp sheets, that she was going to enjoy her stay at St. Anne Manor.

Just then, her eyes glanced toward the desk. Resting on its clean, unused blotter Cary saw the thin, maroon volume. She cried out in bewilderment, then bolted from bed. Her

23

heart pounded as she hurried to see if it was the same book she had so carefully replaced in the hidden drawer. It certainly looked like it.

She saw, upon reaching the desk, that it was indeed the same little book. Prickles of fear ran through her as Cary began to realize the implications of her find. Discovering it freshly laid out on the blotter meant only one thing. Someone had been in her room while she was asleep—an intruder who had moved freely about without her knowledge.

With shaking hands she put the little tome back into its hiding place, then hurried to get dressed. Today, she thought, would be well spent if she got to know her surroundings a little better. Perhaps in that way she'd find an answer to the minor but strangely disturbing mystery.

Cary decided that in order to look around as carefully as she wanted to without creating suspicion she'd need some excuse. Fortunately, as an amateur artist she had the perfect alibi. With her eyes gleaming in eager anticipation, Cary crouched down and pulled her paints, brushes and watercolor block out from under her bed where she had stashed them. It would be nice, she decided, to get back to painting again.

Chapter Five

Once on the ground floor, Cary glanced around. The large, dreary and empty rooms seemed deserted. She wondered if everyone might still be in bed. Then she heard a noise from the kitchen. Hurrying to it, she saw Flora working alone, pounding bread dough. "Good Morning." Cary greeted the woman pleasantly.

"What 'dya want?" Flora glared grumpily at the young woman.

"I'm—I'm sorry to disturb you." Cary wondered if Flora was suffering from a hangover. "But I wanted to know if anyone else was up yet."

"Yeah. Marie's gone t'town an' Janette's out back. The others ain't up though." Upon answering Cary's question, Flora turned her back and stalked off to the far end of the kitchen. Walking away from the slatternly maid, Cary grimaced as she exited through the curtained kitchen door.

At first the yard, glowing gold from the unseasonably intense sun, seemed deserted. Very soon, however, Cary found Janette. Sitting alone on a stone bench out under a lush weeping willow, her plump, drab little body had been almost completely obscured by the tree's long whips of green-gray leaves that hung almost to the ground. She was bending over a bowl set in her lap and seemed oblivious to the girl's approach. As Cary pushed apart the curtain of foliage, however, Janette glanced up.

"Good morning, dear." The old woman uttered her words with the faintest of drawls as she smiled shyly at the young guest. Her eyes fell on Cary's paints and

25

brushes. Patting the empty seat beside her on the bench, she silently invited Cary to join her. "I see you're going to paint," she said.

Cary sat and reluctantly wondered if she ought to offer her help. Janette was shelling peas, and it was a task Cary found almost as intensely boring as washing dishes. It would, however, give her a chance to talk to and get to know the least troublesome inhabitant of the manor, so Cary steeled herself to make the offer. "May I help?" She had the sneaking suspicion that she sounded insincere.

To Cary's intense relief, Janette shook her head. "No, dear," she said, "this is something I can do by myself. Anyway, I know you'd rather paint." She stared curiously at Cary's equipment. "But you've brought no water."

"I brought an empty glass with me. I plan to skim off any water I need from the marsh."

"Be careful or you'll get mud." Janette warned, then smiled nostalgically. "I used to paint too, you know. When I was a young girl, that is."

"Oh really?" Cary looked politely interested.

"Oh, yes. I was quite good actually." The old woman shrugged. "But of course I haven't done it for years." She sighed almost wistfully. "I gave it up when I realized I couldn't go anywhere with it." She faced the girl. "Did you sleep well?"

"Oh yes, very well." Cary decided she had spent enough time talking with Janette. "Nobody'll mind if I explore the grounds, will they? I'd like to find a suitably picture-esque spot to paint."

"Of course you may." Janette's dimples sank into her cheeks once more.

"Do you suppose Charon'll want to come with me later? She can help me explore. She might know of some particularly interesting locations."

"Why don't you ask her?" Janette smiled, then turned her attention to her task of pea shelling once more.

"I would've but she's still asleep."

"You can try when she wakes up, but frankly I doubt if Charon will want to accompany you. She rarely leaves the house anymore." She raised her eyes to Cary's. "Oh, by the way, you needn't bother with the old family mausoleum. I think you'll not only find it locked, but rather ugly."

26

Cary shuddered. "I hadn't the faintest intention of painting any mausoleum."

Janette laughed softly. "You feel that way because you're young. Youth is revolted by the presence of death, whereas age finds comfort in it." The old woman smiled in thoughtful melancholia.

"Oh, I'm sure you're right." Cary rapidly changed the subject because she did indeed find the thought of mausoleums and dead bodies disagreeable. "I guess I'll do a little location hunting on my own right now while I'm waiting for Charon to wake up. See you later."

Janette smiled, and bowed her head in dignified acquiescence as Cary hurried away. "Watch out for quicksand," she added when Cary was almost out of hearing.

Cary wandered down to the edge of high ground where rushes and reeds grew out of the shallows and the land sank into marsh. A few yards beyond stood an ancient cypress. Its gnarled roots grew at strange angles out of the mud. Its thick trunk twisted upward and clumps of moss hung thickly from its branches. When Cary saw it she knew she had to paint it.

As she sat crosslegged on the soggy ground, she forgot that she had intended to use her paints and brushes merely as an excuse to scout out the place. Instead the young woman threw her entire concentration into the image she was creating on the top sheet of her watercolor block. Her mind withdrew from her surroundings as she felt her talent revive after long months of disuse.

Chapter Six

As early morning warmth turned into the blistering heat
of the mid-day, it intruded upon Cary's consciousness. To
escape her extreme discomfort, she packed up her paints
and hurried back to the house. Its thick walls and still
shuttered windows insulated the inhabitants from the
bayou's merciless heat. As Cary rested in her room, waiting for Charon to appear, she enjoyed the relatively cool
air within. She grew to appreciate the value of thick-walled
houses. Air conditioning would have been better, of course,
but at least she felt comfortable.

Growing bored, however, Cary padded down the carpeted hall to Charon's room, knocked, then heard a low
moan. She pushed the door open in alarm and stepped
inside her friend's darkened room.

"Charon, what is it?" Cary ran to the still figure lying
prone on the bed.

Upon looking at the girl's face, Cary gasped. Charon's
eyes were glassy, opened and staring through Cary to
something behind. Cary turned to see the object of her
friend's horrified gaze, but saw only the mirrored vanity-
dresser and stool, a curtained window and a bookcase.

"Charon, what is wrong? Can't you talk?" Cary's tones
were urgent and alarmed.

Charon moaned softly once more, then inhaled a long,
shuddering breath. "Blood!" Her whisper was so soft that
Cary could hardly hear. "On my clothes, on my hands, on
my face!" Charon's features contorted in horror as she

burst into violent trembling. "Aunt Janette found me that way—she washed me off so the others wouldn't know!"

Cary suddenly felt the need to be more capable than she thought possible. "Listen, you're ill. Let me feel your pulse." Taking Charon's wrist, Cary felt its rapid, weak beating against the palm of her hand. Although she had never studied first aid, Cary had picked up from somewhere that sweating, pallor and weak pulse were symptoms of shock. Charon's flesh felt clammy and her pulse indeed fit the description, so Cary felt justified in assuming that if it wasn't shock, her friend's condition might at least be equally serious. "Now lie very still and don't try to get up or anything." As she unconsciously imitated a nurse she had once experienced, Cary's voice became soft but commanding. "You need a doctor, and I'm calling one."

"No! No, please!" Cary winced as Charon's hand cluched hard at her arm, the fingernails digging into her flesh.

"Why not?" Cary grew exasperated. "You're sick, you're probably in shock and I'm not going to sit by and see you grow sicker. I'm calling a doctor." Very gently, she opened Charon's fingers from her arm then pulled away. Closing the door, she left the darkened bedroom then hurried downstairs. She had noticed, without really realizing, a phone set on the table in the large, musty parlor.

"Is anybody around?" Cary called out, hoping to get permission before she took it upon herself to use the phone. "Marie? Janette?" When she received no reply, she picked up the receiver and dialed the operator.

As the woman answered, Cary wondered briefly if small rural telephone districts were run the same way as the large, but she didn't really know.

"Operator!" A woman's flat voice sounded faintly over the line.

"May I have the number I need to dial 'Information' please? I don't have a phone book."

"Information?" The woman sounded openly scornful. "We ain't got no Information. I'm information. Who'd ya want?"

"I need a doctor." Cary's voice shook as she thought of her friend, lying upstairs in a state of shock. "Someone is

29

very sick here and needs help badly. Can you give me the number of one?"

"Only one around here is Dr. Gautier and he's usually out and about."

"This is important. Where can I reach him?"

The operator gave Cary his number then hung up. With trembling fingers, she dialed. After an exasperating ten rings, the phone was picked up. " 'allo?" The loud but quavering voice of a very old, hard-of-hearing woman answered.

"Is Dr. Gautier there?" Cary's heart pounded in anxiety.

"Jed ain't back yet. Won't be back for another couple hours probably." The voice, speaking in a French backwoods drawl, turned interrogating. "Who is this?" Just then, the old woman stopped. "No, wait, I think he comin' in now. Yes, here he is." As the unseen woman handed the receiver to an unseen physician, Cary imagined him to be an elderly man with voice as quavering as the old woman's, for she had assumed that woman was the doctor's wife.

". . . Hello?" The voice of a man broke into Cary's speculations. It was not an elderly voice, but very serious.

"My friend—my friend's very sick." Cary spoke urgently, pleading to the doctor. "I think she's in shock. Her pulse is weak and she's glassy eyed."

"Is she sweating?"

"She feels clammy, and she's hysterical I think." She went on desperately. "Listen, no one else seems to be home and I don't have any way to get her to your office."

"Most of my patients have your same problem," replied Dr. Gautier drily. "Listen, where do you live, and I'll be out as soon as I can."

"About five miles past Fleur-de-Lis, in a house called St. Anne Manor. Do you know where it is?"

There was a brief silence at the doctor's end of the line. "I know where it is," he said quietly. "I'll be right out."

With a sigh of relief, Cary hung up and started to leave the room. As she turned, however, she gasped, for Jerico stood smiling in the doorway. It was a false smile, more of a smirk, that used only the lips while his eyes remained hard and angry. "Oh, you startled me!" cried Cary.

"Did I?" Jerico's sardonic grin remained frozen on his

face as he entered the room. "Aunt Marie wouldn't approve, you know."

"Why not? Charon's very sick."

"Aunt Marie doesn't believe in doctors. She says they're the tools of the devil."

"Well, Marie wasn't here, and I had to do something!" Cary watched in fascination as Jerico slouched across the room to slide into a chair. "Anyway, why would she feel that way? I don't believe you."

Jerico said nothing, but merely looked at her sideways as he tapped one finger to his temple. "They get that way, you know," he finally said.

"Well, I'll answer to Marie when she gets back then. Charon needed help that I couldn't give her." Cary started to sweep out of the room.

"You've heard about that kid in Fleur-de-Lis? The gas station attendant?" Something in Jerico's tone of voice arrested her. The image of the youth's terrified face as he crossed himself at her retreating cab materialized in Cary's memory.

"What about him?" she asked, suddenly apprehensive.

"They found him last night—dead—strangled with his throat cut." Jerico described the event with ghoulish relish.

"Oh that's awful!" Cary shuddered in pity and horror. "Do they know how it happened?"

"Oh, the usual stories—" Jerico shrugged with carefully studied nonchalance. "Ghouls, vampires, ghosts, or possibly a latter day Jack the Ripper. The police department, or what there is of one, is rather dark ages. The villagers have their own theory, of course." He stared at Cary expectantly, waiting for her to ask the obvious question. Instead, she merely raised her eyebrows. That was enough for Jerico. "Do you know what 'loup-garou' means?"

"No." The way Jerico's voice had gone queer when he had pronounced that word made Cary shudder. The word itself had sinister overtones even though Cary didn't understand.

"Loup-garou is French for werewolf. And that's exactly what the villagers think killed poor Pierre. They think the stinking bayou is infested with the beast."

"Oh, that's terrible!" cried Cary in dismay. "Why don't they send those people to school?"

Jerico laughed. "So you don't believe in werewolves?"

"Of course not!"

"So like a lady from the north." Jerico became ironic. "Brought up in sanitized surroundings, in the cold sunlight of crisp winter days, Northern Lady's mind is completely free of such dark terrors. She fails to fear the unknown because she doesn't even know it exists!" Jerico laughed mockingly. "I think you ought to go back there before the loup-garou gets you."

"Well, I suppose you believe in this—this werewolf?" The edge on Cary's voice grew sharper.

Jerico shrugged, then reached nonchalantly into his pocket for a cigarette. He half smiled at her. "Sure I do. I've seen it."

Just then, the sound of car tires crunching on gravel recalled Cary to the needs of the moment. "That must be the doctor now!" She ran eagerly to the front door and let him in.

Chapter Seven

Doctor Gautier proved to be a surprise. From his telephone voice, Cary had imagined a solemn man in his middle fifties. He would be someone with a spreading paunch and an overly serious attitude. She pictured him as having light hair varied by streaks of charcoal gray. His face would be massive, to match a thick set body, and he would probably frown habitually.

Instead, she opened the door on a younger man, one in his late twenties or early thirties. He was tall and gaunt, with a thin sensitive face, piercing black eyes and crisp dark brown hair. Although he didn't scowl, his expression seemed far too serious for a man so young. Still, Cary didn't find his appearance unpleasant—not at all. "Thank you for coming." Cary's voice suddenly became weak as she stepped aside to let him pass. "When I called, your receptionist was afraid you wouldn't be back for hours."

"That wasn't my receptionist, it was my mother. Now, where's the patient?" As he passed her, Cary noticed that he slouched, as if his thin shoulders had been bowed under the weight of too much care and responsibility. The posture was accentuated by his walk—a self-conscious, jerking gait.

"I'll take you to her." Cary hurried up the winding stairs, followed close behind by the young physician. Reaching Charon's door, Cary opened it without knocking. As the light filtered in from the hall, she saw that Charon wasn't in her bed. She stood instead, in front of her vanity-dresser mirror. As the two entered, she didn't move or

33

react, but continued staring at her reflection with frozen horror.

"I thought I told you to stay in bed." Cary spoke sternly.

Suddenly Charon whirled on them, laughing hysterically. "At least I can still see my reflection in the mirror." Her laughter suddenly turned to sobs as Dr. Gautier strode over to her. He slapped her hard with the back of his hand, and she fell silent.

"Now get back into bed." The young doctor spoke quietly as he gently led the mute girl back to her bed. "I'm sorry I had to slap you, but it's impossible to treat an hysterical patient." After taking Charon's temperature and feeling her pulse, he turned to Cary. "I'm going to leave some pills here with you. See that she gets one after every meal and before she goes to sleep. You were right about her condition. She's in shock. If we were closer to a hospital I'd send her."

Suddenly another person burst into Charon's room. It was Marie. "Just what is the meaning of this?" Her cold angry voice cut through the doctor's word's. Both he and Cary glanced up in startled surprise. "Who is this person?" she asked, glaring at Cary.

"Charon fell very ill, so I called in Dr. Gautier."

"By what right did you do that?" Marie swept angrily over to Charon's bed as she stared in cold fury at Cary and the doctor.

"You weren't home and something had to be done for her." Cary felt anger grow inside her. What right had Marie to dictate that Charon be forbidden a doctor? After all, Charon was of age, and presumably mistress of the estate.

"You could have waited until I got back." Marie's voice developed a cold, biting edge.

"I'm sorry, but she couldn't have." Dr. Gautier's voice broke into the two women's with calm command. "Her condition was serious enough to need my help, and her friend did the right thing in calling me."

"Well, you're not to come back. Do you hear?" Marie glared at him. "I won't have a doctor in this house."

Cary could stand it no longer. "Exactly whose house is this?"

"You come down here, impose upon our hospitality, and then have the impertinence to question me?"

"I'm sorry, Marie," replied Cary, "but Charon's health is more important than good manners. I understand that this house and estate belongs to her. Is that correct?"

"Legally yes, but I've been in charge here for fifty years." The old woman replied reluctantly. "I have to be. You can see she's not competent."

"Well then, that settles it." Cary shrugged, bracing herself for the tirade of rage she was sure would follow. "Charon is mistress and has every right to see a doctor if she needs one. I'm sorry Marie, but as Charon's friend—"

The old woman gave an angry curse and swept from the room. She slammed the door savagely. Cary and the young doctor were so dumfounded that they couldn't speak for several long seconds.

"I'm sorry," Cary finally said. "I had no idea she'd create such a scene."

"If you'd known, would you have done any differently?" He watched Cary intently.

Cary shook her head. "I know it's a terribly uncouth thing to do, to defy one of your hostesses, but Charon needed help. Anyway, Marie's attitude toward doctors is totally unreasonable."

"But common enough in these parts." He sighed as he sat down on the stool beside Charon's bed. Cary faced him, herself on its edge. She watched his large and bony but gentle hands give the sick girl an injection. Suddenly Cary felt the need to know a great deal about this sensitive young physician. "Whatever made you choose to practice medicine around here? I mean, it's such a scattered community and the people are so poor."

"All the more reason for them to need a doctor." The young man spoke grimly. "The diseases of poverty are more serious than the diseases of wealth—children with rickets, adults with serious vitamin deficiency. Men and women who look decades older than their years are not in a normal or healthy condition, I assure you."

"But why you, instead of someone else?" Cary studied the serious set of his finely chiseled, intelligent-looking face. Her eyes wandered back to his hands. They were a surgeon's hands, strong looking but with long, sensitive

35

fingers. He could do better than spend his days buried in the backwoods swamp. He hadn't answered the question, so Cary asked again. "Why you?"

He shrugged. "Because I belong here." He answered simply, but his words carried the weight of truth. "I help these people because I came from them. I'm one of them and now that I'm educated I can't turn away. I owe it to them. It's a struggle though—" His voice trailed off and his eyes took on a far away look. "Fortunately I made a few contacts and these send me medicine samples or give me discounts. Most of these people can't afford to pay for their own medicine, nor can I afford to buy it and give it away. I wish I could, but I can't."

"It must be difficult." Cary gazed raptly as the young man revealed himself to her.

"It may get better though." His voice, speaking in a faint echo of the accent Cary had heard from his mother and the gas station attendant, sounded hopeful. "I've applied for a Federal grant to open a clinic—Health, Education and Welfare, you know. It'd be staffed by myself and hopefully by a group of young interns and residents fulfilling their various requirements here instead of in city hospitals." He forced a gloomy chuckle as he stood and prepared to leave. "But of course, even if I get the grant itself, there's still the insurmountable problem of the location. You need a building for a clinic."

The spell broken, Cary followed him to the door. "I hope—I hope it happens for you." Strangely, she felt suddenly shy.

For a second, the young doctor seemed visibly touched, but then he quickly resumed his brisk, almost impersonal tone. "Thank you," he said, "but for now, our main concern is the patient. Keep a close watch on her and don't forget the medicine."

She followed him downstairs, past Marie's frigid stare, then stood in the doorway as he walked out toward his rickety car. As he was about to open the door, however, a sudden question occurred to Cary—something she should have told him earlier. Running toward him, she called for him to wait. He turned and faced her expectantly.

"Doctor, I have to ask you—" Cary gasped breathlessly

from the exertion of running in the heat to where his car was parked.

"Yes, what is it?" He watched her anxiously.

"When I first discovered Charon, she was talking very strangely. She said that when she woke up this morning she was covered with blood." A horrible possibility chilled Cary as she suddenly remembered Jerico's lurid tale about the gas station attendant. "She was merely being hysterical, wasn't she?" Cary asked the last question hopefully.

He regarded her seriously. "What do you think?"

Cary was taken aback. "I—I don't know." As Jerico's almost gleeful rendition of the loup-garou legend came back to her, Cary shuddered. "Did they ever find out who killed that boy?" She asked the question suddenly.

"So you've heard about it too," replied the doctor.

"From Jerico, he's a boy who lives here. I think he's Marie's grand nephew."

"Ah, yes, Jerico!" He spoke the boy's name as if it were already a recognized problem. "And I suppose he told you all the lurid speculations and rumors going around the village? The local superstition that a loup-garou is causing all the disappearances and killings?"

Cary was horror struck. "You don't think—!" Suddenly a bizarre vision of her friend, wandering in a demented state with a bloody arm hanging from her mouth, appeared to Cary, and she felt faint.

"I don't believe that poor sick girl is a werewolf, any more than you do," replied Dr. Gautier. "But that killing and those disappearances were caused by something, you must admit. They couldn't have happened by themselves. I'm not saying that your friend is responsible, but somebody is, and what I'm saying is that it could be she, just as it could be anyone else in the village or surrounding areas."

As Cary shuddered, the young doctor looked earnestly into her eyes. "For your sake, for your friend's sake, watch her closely. If she starts acting strangely, or, God forbid, seems to get worse, call me right away. I'll come around any hour of the day or night. I wouldn't worry though. The pills I gave her should keep her calm until the crisis passes."

Cary murmured her thanks as Dr. Gautier climbed into his car and started the engine. As an afterthought, he turned to her. "By the way, I wouldn't mention her talk about blood to anyone—particularly any villager." She stood in the driveway, watching as he drove away. When she turned toward the grim old house, Cary felt strangely cheerful.

Chapter Eight

The following three days went harmoniously enough. Thanks to Dr. Gautier's pills, Charon spent most of her time asleep. Jerico amused himself by wandering the grounds alone, while Janette, in a touching attempt to befriend Cary, shyly offered to teach her young guest the secrets of Creole cooking.

"A gumbo can either be an okra stew, or a ragout prepared and thickened with gumbo filé." Janette handed Cary the opened spice bottle. "Tonight I'm preparing our gumbo with the filé. Here, smell it."

"Why, it smells like sassafras!"

"That's what it is, mostly, and it's used to thicken the broth. You add it just before the gumbo is to be served, and no sooner. It's very potent."

Marie, her pride insulted by Cary's stand on Dr. Gautier's visit, had locked herself in her room. Her sulking became a sore trial for Janette, who would meekly carry trays of food to her. Her habit was to leave them in the hall after knocking on her elder half sister's closed door. An hour later, she would go back, remove the now empty tray, and take it back to the kitchen.

"Janette, let me carry it up for you. After all, it's because of me that Marie's acting like this." On the first day of Marie's self-enforced solitude, Cary watched guiltily as Janette struggled to carry the food upstairs.

"Oh no," replied the plump, wrenlike woman. "If Marie found out, she'd be furious." Did Cary detect a glimmer of fear in the woman's meek, black eyes?

"That's nonsense," replied Cary. "She has to eat and what does it matter who brings it to her?"

"No, but—" Janette bit her lip. "You've never seen Marie when she was in one of her rages."

"She was pretty mad when she found Dr. Gautier in Charon's room."

"Oh, no, that was nothing. Not one of her *real* rages at least." Janette winced. "They happen rarely, but when they do, I—I become frightened."

Janette had said no more, but hurried up the winding hall stairs to carry lunch to Marie.

After the previous day's excitement had died down, Cary had a chance to think of other things. That afternoon, following a silent lunch, she faced Janette. "Is there a library within reasonable distance of here?"

"Why, no," replied the old woman thoughtfully. "Not other than our own."

"Your own?" Cary's interest surged eagerly. "You mean right here in the house?"

"Why, yes, that large room in the back. We keep it closed for many reasons—partly because of the heat. It has a large south window. Most uncomfortable in summer and if we leave it open, it heats the whole house."

"Does—does it have, I mean, do you know if you have any Latin dictionaries?" Cary stared hopefully.

Janette shrugged. "It may, I don't know. I can give you the key if you like. You're welcome to look for yourself." The woman gazed at Cary curiously. "Why do you need a Latin dictionary?"

Cary explained about the book she had found in her desk drawer, leaving out details of what it was about and how it had reappeared mysteriously.

"How very curious," replied Janette blandly. "I didn't know we had such a book. You must be terribly intellectual to want to spend your time translating a book into English. I'm afraid I'd rather spend my time reading novels."

"I'm afraid it's aroused my curiosity." Cary shrugged.

Janette reached for a ring of keys, suspended from a hook fastened inside a cabinet door. After singling out one large one, she handed the entire ring to Cary. "This black one is the right key. When you're finished and are ready to leave, lock the room again." Janette glanced around in obvious embarrassment. "We have a problem with Flora, you see." She murmured in a low, confidential tone. "She drinks. If we don't keep that room locked, she takes advantage of its isolation to indulge in her vice. We don't encourage her, you know, particularly since she has been known to pass out."

"Why do you keep her on?" Cary winced at the memory of the slatternly, insolent woman.

Janette shrugged. "No one else will work for us. We're isolated, and then there are the superstitions." Janette frowned in painful distaste. Cary remembered Jerico's lurid tales and tactfully let the matter drop.

Hurrying to the library, she let herself in, then closed the door behind her. Janette's description of the room had been correct as far as it went. The large double window faced south, and through it streamed a blazing midday sun. Its rays touched the metal backrest of an old, but good swivel office chair and baked it into a state of unpleasantly burning heat. The air itself was muggy and stale, while specks of dust, illuminated by the bright sunlight, floated freely. On the chair, table, books and shelves had piled yet more dust. It gathered in thick, gray layers.

Cary began her search with the nearest shelf of books. Almost immediately, it became clear to her that some systematic soul had arranged them according to subject matter. Moving from a large but outdated biology section, she reached the shelf holding the history books, then moved on to inspect each row in turn. Finally, after about half an hour, she found the language section. Peering closely, she discovered four books devoted to Latin. One of the four was a dictionary.

The room was sweltering, and she was covered with perspiration and dust. With a sigh of relief, Cary pulled the text down and headed for the door. She was happy to be done. On her way out, she passed a shelf she hadn't needed to search. A few of the titles caught her attention, so Cary stopped a moment to inspect what turned out to be the most well-represented subject in the entire library. Evidently, someone in this old family had been fascinated by the occult, for there were at least six, but often more books on every conceivable topic involving the supernat-

41

ural. She was tempted to take a few of these back to her room too. Deciding first things first, however, Cary let them be. Instead she carried away only the Latin dictionary.

Locking the door behind, she met Janette in the hall. "Did you find what you were looking for, dear?" The dark little woman smiled at her.

"Yes, I found a dictionary," replied Cary. "I hope it's all right for me to take it upstairs, because you were right about the library being uncomfortable."

"Why, certainly. It makes any task more pleasant to be in comfortable surroundings."

During that afternoon and the following, Cary spent her free time trying to translate the *Lycaon*. It was a painfully slow process, because as she tried to recall how each case ending and verb tense affected the meaning, she discovered she knew less Latin than she needed. In school, she had never done too well in the subject, for she had hated it desperately. As she slouched in her desk chair, poring over dictionary pages while fighting an almost irresistible urge to sleep, Cary wished she had been a better student. Only the glimmering suspicion, growing stronger, that the little tome somehow tied in with Charon's condition, kept her going.

The hours spent away from her task of wrestling with that translation, Cary took her duties as combination nurse and pill dispenser very seriously. The third night, Cary, as usual, poured one of the pink pills from its tiny paper envelope. Two landed in her hand. After dropping the extra back where it belonged, she went to the bathroom, poured a glass of water, then carried both glass and pill to her convalescent friend.

"How're you feeling now?" She smiled at the wan, weak girl.

Charon shrugged. "I guess I'm getting better. I feel like reading awhile, but haven't anything new of my own. Did you by any chance happen to bring down any lurid thrillers or hot little romances?" She asked with a wry chuckle.

Seeing that, Cary felt a surge of relief. The dry, humorously sarcastic tones and ironic smile had been Charon's trademarks during those happier days at school. "As a

42

matter of fact, I did. I have a whole suitcase full of English murder mysteries. Sure you feel up to it though?"

"A nice, rational escapist novel sounds exactly what I need." Charon grinned broadly for the first time since Cary had been to the manor. Despite the haggard paleness of her features, she seemed more alive than ever.

"I'll go get it." Cary replied with breathless eagerness. "You take your pill."

"Later." Charon's tone was firm. "But first, a little blood and guts, please."

Cary laughed, returned to her room and hurried back with a particularly involving thriller she had finished on the plane trip down. After leaving her friend propped comfortably in bed against four large pillows, Cary said good night.

With book in hand, Charon returned her farewell.

As Cary reached her own room next to Charon's, she stopped by the door, for within came the sound of stealthy footsteps. Taking a deep breath, she shoved open her closed door. Her hope was to catch and confront the intruder. To her dismay, however, she saw no one. Her room was empty. Cary stepped inside. She felt confused, and yet was sure she had heard something. She glanced around, searching for signs that things had been tampered with.

When her eyes wandered to the bed, she saw a small bulge placed in the center of the mattress under the blanket. She rushed to it, knowing that the lump hadn't been there before. Throwing back the covers, Cary cried out in shocked revulsion when she saw what the blanket was hiding. Spread out on her once clean, now bloodied sheet lay a black cock. Someone had shorn off its comb, tied its claws together and slit its throat. Beside it lay a folded white card.

With shaking hands, Cary reached for it, pulled it away from the dead fowl and opened it. The words had been printed from letters cut individually out of newspapers and magazines. Cary frowned as she read the message, then read it again in disbelief.

> Black cock killed means Death.
> Woe to all who interfere!
> Death your fate, my Dear,

If you choose to remain here.

The card fluttered from Cary's hand as she whirled to face an unknown enemy who threatened her. "You can't scare me into leaving! Not now. I'm staying until I know Charon's out of danger. And furthermore, whoever you are, you write lousy poems!"

With mouth set in anger, Cary threw back the blanket and yanked the edges of the bloody sheet out from under the mattress. She crumpled it around the dead cockerel until she could lift it. Gathering the unsavory load into her arms, Cary started downstairs.

Jerico, who stood at the foot of the steps, stared at her curiously. "What's that?"

"Where are Janette, Marie and Flora?" Cary's voice had an angry edge she didn't bother to hide.

"In the kitchen, clearing up." Jerico continued to stare at her in puzzled bewilderment.

"Come with me. I want you in there too." At Cary's firm command, Jerico followed without speaking.

The swinging door into the kitchen was closed, so Cary pushed bruskly against it with her shoulder. It flew open. The three women, intent upon putting away the dishes, glanced at her then stopped as Cary strode angrily in. "Why, what's the matter?" asked Janette. Marie, who had finally ended her self-imposed exile, stared silently at Cary's load.

"Just this." Cary set the sheet on the floor then spread it open. Marie gasped, while Jerico let out a long, low whistle.

"Where did you get that?" Marie asked sharply.

"It was in my bed. It came with a note ordering me to leave under threat of death." Cary's voice cut cold and angry. "Since we're all assembled here, with the exception of Charon whom I consider above suspicion, I'd like to state that I won't be frightened away like that. I don't know which one of you left me this, but I repeat—I won't be scared away, so forget it!"

"What makes you so sure it's one of us?" Jerico stared at her defiantly. Cary answered coldly.

"Unless you have people hidden away I know nothing about, or unless strangers can tramp into this house and wander about freely, I think the odds are strong that one of you four did it."

They stood in shocked silence. Marie finally brought the matter under control by turning to her grandnephew. "Jerico, get that thing out of here. And you can throw away the sheet."

Jerico obeyed without replying. Cary stared in dazed fascination as he gathered up the bloody fabric that enclosed the limp, dead bird within. Finally he disappeared into the darkness outside the back door.

"I think I'll be going to bed now." Cary turned away. "I don't feel well."

"You'll need clean sheets." Janette bustled after her.

"Never mind, Janette," said Marie. "I'll get them. You finish here." Cary felt mild surprise that Marie had offered to help her. Was it possible that she had grown to feel ashamed of the scene she caused three days ago? She soon found out, however, the old woman's real motives.

As Cary climbed the stairs, she heard Marie follow silently behind. When they reached the linen closet, the woman pulled down a fresh set of white sheets and started toward Cary's room. "Oh, please don't bother." Cary reached for Marie's load. "I can put them on myself. No need to trouble yourself." Her voice sounded stiffly polite and formal for Cary didn't feel comfortable with her companion.

The old woman handed over the sheets to Cary. She stared intently at the girl. Her own black eyes glowed, as if lit from behind, to pierce into Cary's pale blue ones. "The sacrificed black cockerel," she said, "is a threat. Someone wants you out of here, and if I were you, I'd obey. To those who practice voodoo, black roosters symbolize death, and while I don't particularly like you, I'd rather you died somewhere else." After giving Cary this message of good cheer, Marie turned and walked away.

Cary faced her retreating back and repeated, "Threat or no threat, I'm staying until Charon wants me to leave." She backed into her room and closed the door. "Anyway," she murmured, then sighed sadly, "where would I go?"

Chapter Nine

A faint rustle, followed by almost unnatural silence, awakened Cary that night. She lay still in her bed and listened. Shivering despite a merciless heat that poached the muggy swamp land even after the sun disappeared, Cary couldn't be sure that she had actually heard anything at all. It might have been only a dream, for the noise had occurred when she had passed into the borderline between wakefulness and sleep. Cary waited, but the sound seemed to have died out for good. Finally, as the furious pounding of her heart slowed, she prepared to settle back and resume sleep.

Just as she had closed her eyes, however, a faint creaking in the hall jolted her into alert wakefulness. She strained to hear in the darkness, but only that same oppressive silence met her ears.

Suddenly, a shrill scream pierced the heavy darkness. With a gasp, Cary bolted from her bed and ran into the darkened hallway. The voice screamed again. When Cary realized that it came from Charon's bedroom, she ran to her friend's closed door. Throwing herself against it, she turned the knob then lunged inside as the door gave way.

Charon sat upright in bed. The soft glow of moonlight, streaming in through her open window, dimly illuminated her figure. Charon was clutching herself fearfully.

"What happened?" Cary stared in alarm.

"I saw—something!" Her voice gasped breathlessly and quavered. "It was awful! And it touch me!" Her words trailed off into an hysterical choking.

"What's going on?" Marie's firm, commanding question boomed from Charon's doorway. Janette stood behind, wringing her hands in timid concern.

Cary turned toward the stern old woman. "She's had a fright of some sort. I'm still trying to understand exactly what happened."

"Bad dreams." Marie spoke curtly, her thin lips pressed together in cold disapproval. "Too much medicine if you ask me. Those chemicals affect the brain, but no one seems to care, because it makes doctors rich." Marie enunciated the word 'doctors' in a tone of monumental loathing. Marie obviously equated doctors with bedbugs, wanton women, and social diseases. Cary wanted to point out the obvious fact that Dr. Gautier could hardly be considered rich, but she didn't get the chance. After articulating this sweeping denunciation of all medicine, Marie turned sharply and swept from the room. Janette followed. Both Cary and Charon listened, intimidated into silence, as her footfalls faded down the carpeted hall.

When they were completely alone once more, Cary turned to her friend. "Now tell me exactly what happened."

Charon shuddered. "It was awful!" In her fear, she could hardly speak above a whisper. "I'm a light sleeper, you know, and when I felt something move across my cheek, I woke up. The first thing I saw was this—this hand. It was all dry and shriveled up, with long, dirty fingernails. Then I noticed who the hand belonged to." Charon gritted her teeth and shuddered convulsively. "It had the flesh of a mummy—you know, all leathery and shrunked against the bones."

"Go on!" Cary tried to keep her voice calm.

"Well, there it was, and it was touching my cheek!" Charon's voice took on an hysterical edge.

"Was it a man or a woman?" Cary decided that a cool, mundane approach would work best.

"I–I don't know. It was dressed in a shapeless thing— like a robe. It had long, coarse white hair, but it could just as easily have been a man as a woman. It was so shapeless and shriveled."

"I'm surprised you even woke up. That pill was a pretty strong sedative." Cary studied her friend doubtfully.

Charon shrugged. "I didn't take it. I felt good when I

47

turned out the light, and calm, so I decided I could get along without it. I'm glad I did! The thought of that—that *thing* touching me and me not knowing—" Charon broke into another spasm of shuddering.

"What happened then?" Cary spoke briskly as she evaluated the possibilities. Either Charon was imagining the whole thing, or else something had really been in the room with her. Since she claimed she had actually felt something touch her, Cary was inclined to believe her—particularly after her own peculiar experience with the *Lycaon*.

"After you woke up and screamed, what became of this person?"

Charon bit her lip in bewilderment. "Why, I don't know. It just sort of disappeared."

"Well, would you've noticed if it had escaped through the door?"

"It didn't. I'm sure of that." Charon spoke with conviction. "It backed away from me, toward the window, then headed for some shadows over *there*." She pointed to her right, where a corner, unlit by the window's moon-illumination, converged into darkness. In that corner had been set her mirrored vanity-dressing table and a chair.

"Then the thing must still be here!" Cary wasn't really sure what she'd do if she actually found someone because she knew she'd probably have to cope with any situation alone. The two old women would be even less helpful than the girl lying in bed, and she certainly knew better than to count on Jerico's coming to her aid.

As Charon obediently pulled down the lamp chain, a dim but adequate light flooded into all corners of the room. At first glance, Cary saw nothing. Where inky shadows had previously blotted out her view, she saw now clearly the dresser, Charon's overstuffed arm chair and a short expanse of busy, flowered wallpaper. No thorough search was needed to confirm that the intruder was nowhere in the room. Cary turned to her still shivering friend.

"Are you sure it wasn't just a dream?"

Charon shook her head. "Those cold, dry fingers I felt couldn't possibly have been my imagination." She spoke with frightened conviction.

Cary glanced over at the large French window. A sudden suspicion gripped her. "Charon," she whispered, "turn off your light for a moment!"

When the room fell dark, she padded silently to that window and peered out. Extending from Charon's room, like all the others on the second floor, was a balcony. Cary had hoped, or rather feared, that whatever Charon saw might have taken refuge out there. The balcony, however, was empty.

Just as she was about to turn away, her eyes caught a movement on the grounds below. She gasped, for slipping into the darkly grown marsh just beyond the manor grounds, Cary saw a dimly outlined form. Before it disappeared, her eyes caught glimpse of its shroudlike gown and trailing white hair.

"What is it?" Charon's half whispered question came out as a whimper.

"I saw it too!" Cary's head pounded and her mouth went suddenly dry. "It's out there at the edge of the cypress grove!"

Chapter Ten

"Cary, what're we going to do?" Charon's question was a little more than a terrified whisper. "There's a—a thing running loose around here, and we're helpless."

"It's still not too late for you to come away with me to Los Angeles." Cary gazed anxiously at her friend.

"I can't." Charon spoke those words with grim finality.

"Why not?" Cary's angrily voiced question burst explosively from her. "You talk about how you're bound to this place, but sometimes I think you stay because you like to suffer."

Charon sighed. "I'll tell you the real reason, and frankly you'll be shocked by how crass I've become. I have one more month to go before I can leave. The conditions of the will under which I inherit the estate specify that I have to live here for a period of no less than five years. I've been here four years and eleven months already, and believe me—it's seemed like forty years. If I fail to stay, I'll lose not only St. Anne Manor but everything else as well—the stocks, the bonds and the money. If that happens, the entire estate is to go toward the financing of a museum commemorating my family and its history!" Charon gave a short bitter laugh.

"Oh, Charon, how awful!" Cary gasped. "You mean you'd get nothing?"

"Nothing!" replied Charon grimly. "So you see now why I can't leave yet. It's not only for myself, although I admit I want what's coming to me, but for Marie and Janette. They're old women. Where would they go if I lost the place? I couldn't see them turned out into the cold. I feel as if they're members of the family." Charon slapped her hand over her mouth to stifle the rising tide of hysterical sobbing. "I feel so trapped!"

"Can't you find a loophole? I mean, certainly the National Bank and Trust of New Orleans—"

"They've tried, God knows they've tried, but the will's iron clad. It was all right at first, but then these horrible things started happening." Charon couldn't go on. Her face working, she turned away and let herself sink stomach down onto her bed. Her shoulders hunched forward with forearms pressed into her chest. She hid her face with open palms which she cupped upward so that the backs of her hands rested on a pillow. Cary hesitated a minute, then decided to act.

"Charon, you're a bundle of nerves. I'm going downstairs and make you a cup of hot cocoa. If you need me, call out and I'll come running."

When Charon didn't reply, Cary hurried out of the room. Flicking on the dim hall light, she hurried down the steps, across the ground floor to the kitchen. Alone and surrounded by old but serviceable appliances, shiny enameled walls and starched window curtains, Cary felt really comfortable for the first time since she had come to St. Anne Manor.

She paused for a second to admire the polished copper pans that hung from a ceiling beam. Strings of garlic and pepper attached there also added a pleasantly ornamental touch. She hurried to the refrigerator and pulled out a carton of milk. Grabbing one of the smaller saucepans, she filled it half full.

Humming cheerfully, Cary lifted the cardboard box filled with large wooden oven matches from its place on a shelf. She extracted one, scraped it against the sandpaper strip attached to its side, then applied the flame to one burner as she turned on the gas. With a soft puff of released energy, the tiny jet fed into a controlled circle of flames over which Cary set the pan of liquid.

At first the fire flickered too high and promised to burn the milk, so Cary turned the corresponding burner now to 'low'. While she waited for it to simmer warm, she went to the cupboard and pulled out a can of powdered cocoa and

51

some sugar. These ingredients she mixed with the heating liquid.

After testing it with her finger, Cary poured cocoa into two large mugs, then carried one in each hand up the steps to the second floor.

"Well, I'm back." She announced cheerfully as she re-entered her friend's room. Setting her mugs down on the bed table, she studied Charon with concern. The girl was sitting now, propped against her pillows in a slouched, morose pose. She neither moved nor answered when Cary entered, but continued to stare unblinkingly at an unseen point somewhere ahead.

"Here, drink this." Cary wedged the tumbler of cocoa between the thumb and fingers of Charon's left hand. The girl, feeling its presence, clutched at it. She pressed its rim against her lips.

Suddenly Cary heard a creaking of weight upon settled wood. It sounded to her as if it came from the floor below. Charon heard it too, because her head whipped left to face Cary. "What was that?" Her face grew even paler.

"I heard it too!" Cary jumped to her feet and ran toward the door.

"Be careful!"

Cary didn't hear Charon's warning as she hurried to the hallway. The light still shown. She started down the flight to the first floor, and then it happened.

About the fifth step from the top, the carpet, which had been previously tacked securely to the wood underneath, gave way. It catapulted Cary forward with a scream frozen on her lips. She plunged through space, her arms flailing helplessly. At that precise instant, the hall light went out to leave her in total darkness. Cary heard the aspirated words, "I warned you!" They came from the hall below—a voiceless cry of triumph as she fell.

Chapter Eleven

As her body whipped around in a ninety degree turn, Cary thrashed wildly. Throwing herself toward the bannister as her body continued its downward tumble, Cary flung her arms over its cool, polished wood surface. As her weight settled, her armpits scraped uncomfortably. Nevertheless, it hooked her securely. Although she slid a few more steps, Cary's near fatal descent had been checked by what seemed to her a near miracle.

"Charon!" Cary's breathless voice seemed barely audible as she gasped out the name of her friend. From above, in the darkness, she heard Charon's footsteps running toward the stairway.

"What is it?" Charon sounded anxious as she reached its summit.

"Stay where you are!" Cary cried out as she saw her friend start down.

Charon stopped. "Well, at least let me turn on the light. No wonder you fell!" She clicked on the switch so that the gloomy rays from a single thirty watt bulb illuminated the hall. "I'd have fallen too, wandering around in the dark like that." She extended her foot to descend.

"Charon, stay!" Cary gasped the command hoarsely as she disentangled herself from the bannister. Her breath came hard and painful, but not so much as when her chest had first slammed into the railing. "The carpet—" She let herself slump into a sitting position on the nearest step. "Someone untacked it—just now. It wasn't loose when I went to fix our chocolate. I'm sure of that!"

"Then that noise?" Charon stared in horror.

"I don't know what caused it." Cary replied grimly. "However, the light was on when I started down the stairs. It went off only after I—"

"What's going on here?" Marie's stern voice interrupted their conversation. It grew louder as the old woman hurried down the hall toward Charon. "This is hardly the hour to—Oh!" She had been about to reprimand both severely until she saw Cary slumped on a step below several yards of loosed carpeting.

"My goodness, what happened?" Marie sounded genuinely shocked and distressed.

"Someone, for reasons unknown," said Cary evenly, "loosened the stairway carpeting. I heard a noise and went down to investigate, lost my footing when the rug shot out from under my feet, and I was very nearly killed or injured."

"How awful!"

From out of the gloom on the opposite side of the upstairs hall emerged Janette. As she hurried toward them, she tied the belt of her housecoat. Her long gray-black hair, braided into hanging plaits, and her scrubbed round face lent her appearance a strangely girlish quality as she twittered and crooned in gentle distress. "Has there been an accident?" She stared at Cary in what seemed to be horror. "Are you hurt?"

"I think I'm all right," replied Cary weakly. "I'm sure I've developed a few nasty bruises, but I don't think there are any bones broken."

"How did it happen?" Janette stared in fascination at the loose carpet. "It was always so securely fastened. I'm sure of it."

"Someone loosened it," replied Cary grimly.

"Are you quite sure?" Marie sounded almost insulted at the idea.

"I'm positive. It was all right awhile ago. Rugs don't come unfastened so easily that a whole stairway runner accidentally works loose within the space of half an hour."

Marie pressed her lips together and frowned, then glanced doubtfully to her younger half sister. "I can't imagine—"

"Who sleeps downstairs? Anyone?" Cary peered at both

sisters. "It happened after I started to check on a noise I heard from down there."

"Flora and Jerico both sleep downstairs." Charon almost cried out the fact as its significance hit her suddenly. "Why, either one of them—"

"Jerico would do no such thing!" Marie angrily interrupted Charon. "He may have foolish ideas, but he's not vicious."

Sure, that's what they all say, thought Cary cynically. She imagined that juvenile courts were full of women, all of whom insisted their hoodlum sons, grandsons and nephews were 'good boys'; however, Cary had the tact to keep her thought to herself. "Well, what about Flora?"

"Flora's probably passed out drunk by this time." Janette nodded her head knowingly.

"Janette!" Marie scolded her sister in a shocked, angry voice. "What a thing to say!"

"My dear Marie, you know as well as I that I speak the truth. Flora is a drunkard, but she's the only servant we can get to live here with us."

Cary felt surprise that the birdlike little woman had asserted herself so strongly.

"Well, that may be, but I don't care to hear another word of such talk." She turned to Cary and Charon once more. "If you're all right, I suggest we all return to bed. It's been a trying evening and I, for one, need my sleep. Good night." Marie disappeared into the darkness as she headed toward her own room. Janette followed after, leaving the two young women alone.

Charon remained standing above the stairs as Cary climbed gingerly over the loosened rug to the second floor. As she reached her friend's side, she noticed the haunted gaze of horror in the girl's eyes. "Charon, what is it?" She touched Charon's shoulder anxiously. "What's the matter?"

"The house!" Charon replied hollowly. "The house has transferred its wrath to you. It was after me before, but now that you're here, it wants you instead. It's going to kill you!"

"What are you talking about?" Cary replied in exasperation.

"I feel that houses take on the character of those who live within them." Charon turned urgently to her friend.

55

"Generations of evil have existed here, Cary, and they made the house itself evil."

"I suppose the house can speak out loud." Cary retorted sarcastically then recounted to her friend the whispered words she had heard.

Charon's eyes widened. "I heard the words, 'Get out, Pretender' the day I found the black widow spider in my bed. I looked around but couldn't find who spoke. And then the night a bronze statuette we kept in the hall landing table fell when I was standing below, I heard the words, 'You die'. That figurine barely missed me, and it would've killed me if it hadn't."

"Oh Charon!" Cary felt wave after wave of horror wash over her. "What are we going to do?"

Chapter Twelve

Sunlight, streaming cheerfully through the window, woke Cary the following morning. If it hadn't been for her muscles, sore and stiff from her fall, she would have laughed at the previous night's horror. Instead, she shivered, knowing that her fears were indeed based on reality.

Her head rolled toward the right as she silently watched her friend sighing in sleep. After the accident, both had been too scared to sleep alone, so Cary had joined Charon in her large double bed.

All the excitement had exhausted the fragile girl. She showed signs of remaining unconscious for hours. Cary, however, couldn't stand to remain in bed any longer for her mind buzzed with unanswered questions. She sat, swung her legs out from under the coverlet, and stood. Yawning, she wandered to the window and stared out at the surrounding bayou.

Leaving her friend's room, Cary formulated the day's plan. She dressed quickly, throwing on a sleeveless cotton dress. On her desk, still opened from her attempt at translation, was the *Lycaon*. With a sigh of acidic frustration, Cary slammed it shut. She was no Latin scholar and knew she could never hope to understand what was printed there. It suddenly seemed pointless. But she would try one more time later. For now, however, she had other things to do. Cary hoped to reach Dr. Gautier and find out what he knew about her friend, her friend's family, and the strange trio living under the same roof.

Suddenly a thought burst upon her. Since doctors study

Latin in order to qualify for their degrees, perhaps Dr. Gautier could read the book if she took it to him. Sighing in exultant relief, Cary stuck it into her oversized cloth handbag.

Finally Cary was ready to leave Charon a note and be off. She had no intention of letting her friend know the real reason for her errand, so she had to formulate an excuse. Hurrying into Charon's room, she grabbed paper and pencil off the writing table.

Dear Charon,
Am feeling painfully sore this morning. Have gone to see Dr. Gautier and find out about possible breakage. He may at least be able to give me something stronger than aspirin to see me through the mending period. See you later.

Cary

After folding the note and leaving it on the table, Cary hurried out and down the steps. She trod quietly to the parlor. A silence, almost eerie, hung oppressively throughout the place, but she reflected that the two old sisters, tired from the night's excitement, had probably slept late. Cary hurried to the phone and dialed. Within five rings, the young doctor's mother answered, her hoarse voice inflecting with a questioning tone.

"Is Dr. Gautier in?" Cary suddenly felt a guilty clutch at her throat. Why bother him for something so obviously a private family matter? Cary was about to apologize and hang up when his voice broke into her thoughts. "Yes?"

Cary bit her lip. "Doctor, this is Cary Matthews at St. Anne Manor. I'm sorry to be such a nuisance, but something happened."

"What?" His voice became terse and anxious.

"Can—can I meet you somewhere? It's not something I feel free to talk about over this telephone."

"I can come out there if you wish." His calm, strong manner soothed Cary, and she felt thankful that she had called.

"No—no, it's best discussed in privacy. Perhaps you know of somewhere other than here."

"Do you mind walking?"

"Not really," replied Cary.

"Take the dirt road that runs past the estate—the one you must have traveled over when you passed through Fleur-de-Lis. Walk back toward the village. About a mile and a half from St. Anne Manor you'll reach a spot where the road curves. I'll meet you there."

Cary hung up, stepped into her shoes and hurried toward the front door. The sense of relief at escaping the musty house exhilarated her. Outside, humid but fresh air warmed her as she walked down the driveway. An intricate pattern of lights and shadows from the sun mottled the overgrown lawn. Only the muted buzzing of insects, birdcalls, and an occasional splash interrupted the silent calm.

Dr. Gautier called it a dirt road. As Cary walked along, however, shaking off the viscous goo that clung to her shoes, she understood that to call the mud path a road, or to describe it as dirt was merely wishful thinking. As she approached the curve, however, all Cary's thoughts flew forward to the battered Nash that idled in waiting for her. She called out an eager greeting, then loped toward it, her heart lurching in joy.

The young doctor leaped from the car, ran over to the passenger door and pulled it open. His exaggerated good manners surprised her, especially since, thanks to Bob, she had grown used to casual, almost crude informality. "Oh, you don't have to bother opening my door like that." She smiled gratefully.

The young man's expression grew confused, ill at ease. "Have I done something wrong?"

Cary felt a pang at the sight of his troubled face. "Oh no, not at all! I guess I've just grown used to bad manners. You surprised me." As she slid into the tattered front seat, she caught glimpse of the troubled expression in his deep black eyes. She smiled again, trying to put him at ease. "Thank you. You're very nice." He slammed the door and hurried around the front to join her inside.

As he sat behind the wheel, Cary turned. "I'm sorry to trouble you like this." She spoke ruefully. "But I really don't know anyone else I can turn to. The situation at the manor has become so sticky."

"I understand." He replied quietly. "What happened now?"

Cary recounted the events of the previous night as he listened quietly. She wasn't so wrapped up in her story that she failed to notice the frown creasing his forehead, or the grim set to his lips as he stared through the windowshield.

"You could have been killed." When he finally spoke, his quiet voice cut through Cary like a razorblade.

She shrugged. "So could Charon or either of the old ladies."

"Yes, it might have been anyone." He turned to her, gazing earnestly. "Do you realize how many people have died from falling down stairs? I ought to take you right back to my office and make sure you're all right. You've probably injured yourself."

"No, I feel fine—just a little muscle soreness is all. But the real point is, we don't know who did it or why. Was it merely a sick, stupid trick to scare me, or was it a genuine attempt at murder? Charon and the two old ladies were upstairs when I fell, so the noise and those awful words must've come from the two people sleeping downstairs."

"Who does that leave?"

"Flora, that dreadful old lady who keeps house, and Jerico."

"Jerico again." Dr. Gautier pressed his lips together. "He's a troubled boy—but is he a murderer? Or a potential murderer?"

"That's the question. Flora's a seemingly harmless old soak, so he's my ripest suspect right now. But how can we find out? He used to attend the Le Beau Military Academy in Baton Rouge until he got expelled. What did he do that was so awful? As I understand it, this hasn't been the first school to kick him out."

"It should be easy enough for me to check." The young physician frowned as if trying to make a decision. He paused a second, then spoke. "I guess I ought to tell you what I've learned about everyone you're staying with. Some of it's questionable, but even so, forewarned is forearmed as the old cliché goes."

Cary waited silently.

"First of all," he began with a sigh, "your lovely, tragic friend Charon is the last known descendant of a family that terrorized this part of the country for over a hundred years. She is a Parveau on her mother's side—a family notorious for its fondness for cruelty and violence."

"Ooooohh, how melodramatic!" Cary giggled in spite of his seriousness. She stopped suddenly, however, when she saw the pained expression on his face. "But really, Charon's not like that at all!"

The young man shrugged. "Perhaps her father, being a Yankee stranger with fresh heredity rather than a blood relative, saved her. The point is, what I'm telling you is not a ghost story, Miss Matthews, but a more or less true background and history of the family that inhabited St. Anne Manor." He sighed, staring gloomily out the window.

"Go on!" Cary urged eagerly.

After a pause, he continued. "The beginnings are shrouded in the mist of legend, but it seems to be a generally acknowledged fact that the early Parveaus were decadent French nobility who had been saved from imprisonment only by edict of the king himself. Even so, clemency came only on condition that they leave France, which happened immediately thereafter. They ended here in Louisiana and built the original St. Anne Manor, which served as combination estate and plantation.

"Almost immediately, rumors spread concerning their practice of slave torturing. These rumors grew stronger, if anything, until the Civil War finally outlawed human bondage.

"Throughout the history of St. Anne Manor, stories of black masses and satanic rites had spread among nearby villagers—although no doubt exaggerated. During times when these rumors were strongest, young women disappeared—sometimes to be found later with their throats slit. There may have been no connection, of course, and there's no way of verifying anything as absolute fact up to this point."

Cary shivered, but remained silent as the doctor continued his narrative.

"Although these rumors may be unconfirmed, you won't get anyone from Fleur-de-Lis or surrounding areas to regard them as anything but gospel truth. The incontestable facts, however, are the events that have occurred within recent history and in front of witnesses. Miss Charon's great-grandfather Louis got drunk one night and stabbed

61

his wife Sophie—the beautiful young woman who had been carrying his child for eight months. After it happened, someone in the household sent for the nearest doctor. By the time he reached her, however, Sophie was already beyond help. On the chance that the child inside might still be alive, the doctor took a knife and cut open the dead woman's belly. He pulled out a baby girl—a delicate creature who survived her premature birth only because of constant attendance and incredible good luck."

"What happened to her?"

"Little Lucie spent her early youth at the Manor. Louis had other children, sons older than her by his first wife, but he loved his youngest daughter best because she reminded him of her mother whom he loved passionately. Lucie probably died very young because she disappeared, to all accounts, when she was fifteen.

"About six years after her birth, he brought in three young quadroon children, a pair of sisters and a boy, to take care of Lucie and act as companions. The eldest of the two servant children tended both Lucie and her own sister who was then only a three-year-old child. The boy was older than the girls and ran away when he was in his teens."

"Janette and Marie!"

"Probably." Dr. Gautier shrugged. "Shortly thereafter, old Louis, who had become crippled with syphilis, hanged himself to nobody's grief. A few years later, Lucie disappeared."

"What was she like? Does anyone know?"

"All Parveau's children were a little strange, but Lucie was always considered a little more peculiar than her half brothers. The condition was probably caused by the unusual circumstances surrounding her birth, or quite possibly due to inbreeding. Sophie, her mother, was Louis's second wife but his first cousin."

"Where does Charon fit into all this?" Cary felt bewildered.

"I really don't know, because at this point all the facts evaporate again. After Louis, the Parveau stock dwindled quite suddenly, but one of his children managed to sire a child healthy enough to grow up and marry a Yankee stranger."

"Charon's father!" Cary remembered her friend talking about how he died in war.

"I'm telling you all this because I feel your friend is a nice girl being victimized by an evil that existed in that place long before she was ever born."

"But what can I do?"

Dr. Gautier sighed. "I don't honestly know, but I would venture to guess that whatever is going on at St. Anne Manor is centered around that girl. It's aimed against her in one way or another. Those stairs may have been meant for her, not for you."

"But the warning—it was a death threat."

The young physician nodded gravely. "True, it's connected, but secondary as far as the would-be murderer is concerned. You stand between him and your friend. Whoever wrote that note wants you out of the way to get at her. I don't think it mattered which one of you slipped on that stairway. The ultimate goal is to destroy her, but if it becomes necessary to kill you—" his voice trailed off as he became absorbed in unpleasant thought.

"Yes, I've felt that too." Cary stared at him pleadingly. "You will help, won't you? I'll try not to be a nuisance, but—"

"You're no nuisance!" As Dr. Gautier stared at her warmly, Cary blushed and drew in her breath too sharply.

The young physician reacted by tensing himself consciously. He directed his gaze away from her toward the muddy scenery beyond his windshield, and Cary realized he was shy. Self-annoyance welled in her as she realized she had embarrassed him by overreacting.

She tried to break the slightly uncomfortable silence that followed. "I want to thank you. I feel much better knowing there's someone I can turn to if things get nasty." Another silence ensued until Cary remembered the *Lycaon*. "Oh, by the way, can you read Latin?"

"A little." He replied with a dry chuckle. "It was never my favorite subject."

Cary pulled the little book out and handed it to him. "Could you look this over if you have time, please? It may be important." She explained how she had found it placed on top of her desk in a most unexplainable manner. He took the little tome, glanced at it with grave curiosity, then placed it on the seat beside him.

"Listen," he said, "when you go back, find some excuse to look over the whole house. Get to know the entrances, stairways and dumbwaiters if any. Check for heavy chandeliers that might come crashing down, or any other danger spots. Familiarize yourself with the entire house. Such knowledge might save you later. And whatever happens, don't let on what you're doing to anyone."

"Not even Charon?"

"Especially not to Charon. I doubt that she's in any condition to keep your secret if someone skillful pumps her for information. Anyway, you'd only create fear or resentment, and frankly you don't need either."

Cary smiled her farewell and started out the car. "Oh yes, and by the way," continued the young doctor. "If you need something, don't go to Fleur-de-Lis. Get someone to drive you into Banting. It's just a few miles farther and much safer."

Cary stopped. "What's wrong with Fleur-de-Lis?"

"Those children they've lost lately—it's understandable that they've gotten hysterical, I guess. They blame it all on St. Anne Manor. They'll know you're from there and frankly it might be dangerous for you."

"Okay, I understand." Cary replied cheerfully.

"Good. I'll call you as soon as I hear anything about Jerico, but in the meantime, for God's sake, be careful!"

"I will. Bye for now." As she bade farewell, Cary smiled sympathetically into his eyes. She caught a fleeting warmth in his own. As he returned her farewell almost wistfully, Cary longed to reach out and touch his hand. She wanted to look him in the eye and say, "Listen, I like you a lot. Don't be afraid of me." But she couldn't. The recent humiliation she had suffered because of Bob, though fading, still was enough to make Cary hesitate.

Chapter Thirteen

When Cary returned to St. Anne Manor, she realized that for all practical purposes she was quite alone. She hurried up to her own room, careful to move silently. She didn't want to disturb Charon, who remained languishing in bed, or arouse anyone else who might interfere. After grabbing a pencil and note pad from her desk, for she didn't entirely trust her own memory, Cary began her inspection.

Altogether it seemed to be a straightforward enough old house. The central stairway led up onto a second floor hallway. The balcony overlooking the ground level was the spot under which Charon had nearly met her death the time someone had dropped a bronze statuette from its ornate mahogany railing. "Definitely a danger spot," murmured Cary. She now appraised the house with a fresh perspective.

In the deserted kitchen Cary made a most enlightening discovery. Behind a door she had assumed led to a kitchen closet, she found another flight of steps. These were narrower and darker than the main staircase and obviously were used by servants. The existence of this staircase broadened her list of suspects. Anyone could have moved freely from floor to floor last night without her ever suspecting. Since both old women must have known of it, she wondered why neither had mentioned the fact. Why had they allowed her to choose between Jerico and Flora as the only possible culprits? She wondered why Charon herself hadn't said anything. She had, after all, lived in the house for almost five years. She must have discovered them herself long ago.

Taking a deep breath, Cary climbed up the hidden steps. They led to a door on the second floor. Opening it, she stepped out into the northern end of the upstairs hallway. She had noticed earlier the battered door out of which she had emerged, but had assumed it led only into a broom closet. Cary decided, then and there, to avoid all further assumptions.

Down the hall was Janette's bedroom. Having decent inhibitions against undue snooping, Cary hesitated. She reminded herself, however, of the doctor's warning that in the future, her own and Charon's survival might depend on precise knowledge of their surroundings. Taking a deep breath, Cary knocked softly.

"Come in." Janette's mild voice answered and Cary's mind raced to find something suitable to say as she pushed open the door.

"I–I just wanted to find out how you were feeling after the shock you must've had last night." It sounded feeble, but vaguely valid, for her to inquire after the old woman's health.

"Oh, I'm fine. After all, I wasn't the one in danger." Janette's face dimpled into her sweet smile.

Janette's pleasant room reflected her personality. Pink and gray polished cotton curtains, edged with ruffles, contrasted pleasantly with the white walls. The furniture was antique but comfortable looking. The chairs were as wide and soft as Janette herself, the bed deep, and the dresser and writing table serviceable. Though cluttered with ceramic knick knacks and figurines, Janette's room was basically neat. It took only a rapid glance for Cary to determine that it contained nothing of interest.

"I just wanted to check is all." Cary backed away.

As Janette thanked her politely, the young woman closed the door. However foolish she may have felt, she had nevertheless accomplished her purpose.

Hurrying on, she passed her own and Charon's room to stop before Marie's. After receiving no answer to her knock, she tried the door as she had done with Janette's. Marie's room, however, proved to be locked. She reflected, without surprise, that Marie was a fiercely private, strangely reactionary person who would trust no one—not even in her own home. For one wild second, Cary considered picking the lock, but decided against it. She didn't really know, after all, when Marie was coming back. It would be hideously embarrassing to be caught breaking in.

Downstairs, Cary found nothing she hadn't noticed before, so she quickly went outside. She had never really gotten around to exploring the grounds before, and now she had her chance.

She hurried across the sodden lawn to the point where grass gave way to weeds. Through those had been beaten a narrow mud path. Cary followed as it led down the strangely sunken land.

As she passed through a stand of thickly grown cypress, the path curved. Beyond the crook, it veered left. At its terminus had been built an unexpected structure. The windowless white brick edifice had been shaped in the same architectural style as the main house itself; however, its size was many times smaller. As Cary approached the gloomily ornate entrance, she felt suffocated. This then, she guessed, was the Parveau mausoleum.

On either side of its bolted iron door stood an empty urn. Each had been carved out of a white stone Cary didn't recognize. The whole building had been set upon a cement slab into which well worn steps had been built. As Cary slowly climbed them, her skin crawled in the eerie sensation that something was watching her.

The rusty iron lock remained intact as Cary yanked on it. Were it to give way, she didn't really intend to enter the gloomy sanctum of the manor's dead, but would have just peered inside. Suddenly hearing a soft chuckle from behind, Cary whirled guiltily.

"We always keep those doors locked. It's the family mausoleum, you know." Jerico's soft voice taunted her with its hint of amused irony. He studied her with a curious half-smile.

"I–I wasn't really—that is to say, I had no intention—" Cary stammered in embarrassment. "It's just that I never saw this building before, and I wanted to get a better look."

Jerico laughed softly. "No need to apologize. It's not *my* family resting spot. I could care less. Anyway, they don't keep it locked because they're afraid of people breaking

67

into it. Frankly, they're more concerned with keeping what's inside from getting out."

Suddenly Cary thought she heard a low moan from within. Fear prickled her flesh. "Oh, Jerico, sometimes you give me the creeps!" Cary spoke nervously, almost angrily as she hurried down the steps and planted her feet once more on the ground. A shiver passed through her and it was a reaction that annoyed Cary almost more than the nonsense that inspired it.

"I'm sorry." Jerico's voice was changed, humbled now as he stood staring at her sadly. "I didn't really mean to. You've been really decent to me, considering how I've acted and what you probably think I've done."

Cary looked at the gangling adolescent and softened. "I know," she said, smiling. "But you musn't go around trying to scare people the way you do. I know it's fun for you when someone reacts, but someday somebody might take your words seriously."

"What if they do?" Jerico shrugged.

"You go around talking about ghosts and werewolves and things—well, I don't believe in them, but then again I'm not a poor, uneducated soul who's spent his entire life in these creepy surroundings. The things you dwell on can create fear, Jerico, and fear can become an ugly force. Fear can cause the same horror usually credited to the imaginary demons that inspired it. Look at the Spanish Inquisition or the witch hunts of Salem."

"I'm not afraid—"

"That's not the point. Someone else might act foolishly because of you. If you're in the way, you might get hurt."

"I can take care of myself."

Cary smiled pityingly at Jerico's blustering. It had been years ago that she and her friends had gone through what he was experiencing now. Being around him made her feel suddenly old. "Oh, Jerico!" Cary cried out in exasperation.

"Can I walk with you?" The youth stared at her eagerly, with pleading eyes.

"Of course you can," replied Cary. They walked along in silence. After about ten minutes, Jerico spoke. "I'm sorry about all the bad things that've happened to you since you've been here. Really I am."

Cary wondered what it was, if anything, he was about to

confess. She walked along in silence, waiting for him to continue.

"I mean, you've been nice to me even though I've been rotten, and you stood up to Aunt Marie. Somebody has to, I mean. But I want to tell you, I didn't leave that dead bird in your bed."

"Thank you, Jerico." Cary wasn't sure that was the appropriate reply, but could think of nothing more to the point.

After a few minutes of silence, the boy spoke again. "You're much prettier than Charon."

"She's been ill. You should've seen her at school when she was herself. She was first runner up in the college varsity queen contest."

"If you had entered, you'd have been queen." Jerico spoke with an intensity that alarmed Cary. Glancing at him out of the corner of her eye, she wondered if he were developing a crush on her. She dreaded that possibility because her situation was already sticky enough without that. Aloud she spoke rather drily. "I heartily doubt it. I'm not the beauty contest type."

"Why didn't you ever get married?" Jerico asked the prying question in the candid manner of a child.

"Oh Jerico!" Cary's mind, with its processes hidden from the youth by her false heartiness, flashed back to Bob's smiling face. She could think about him now without pain raking her insides. To her surprise, however, a second face replaced his, a face—Cary immediately broke off thinking about that face. She was foolish to have such ideas about a man she hardly knew. It was as childish as the moon eyes Jerico now directed at her.

Cary laughed out loud, hoping she could hide the hurt she felt whenever someone asked that hateful question. The ruse, she decided, had been successful when she glanced at Jerico and saw that he stared at her with abashed bewilderment. "What's so funny?" He asked.

Cary retorted drily. "You sound like my mother."

Jerico said nothing, but merely scowled.

"Now what's the matter?" Cary took pity on him.

"You're making fun of me."

"No, I'm not." She replied sincerely. "It's just that you shouldn't ask awkward questions."

"I'm sorry." Jerico sighed dolefully. "It seems that I'm always asking bad questions, or unintentionally insulting people, or bringing up subjects that they'd rather not think about."

"Tact develops with age, Jerico. You're too young to appreciate the practical value in avoiding unpleasantness."

"I'm not all that young!" Jerico spoke defensively.

"No, I'm not saying you're a child." Cary tried to soothe the boy's ruffled feelings. "It's just that you're intense. Very intense people who care too strongly about something often forget that certain things are best left unsaid or glossed over."

"You're wrong," he replied. "Things—especially things concerning evil—should be brought out into the open where light can shrivel it away."

"It doesn't always works like that," replied Cary grimly. "Sometimes you discover you've cornered a force you can't control when it fights back. Sometimes it can even kill you." Cary's mind flashed back to her experience of the night before.

"I'll take my chances." Jerico replied with naive confidence.

"And maybe endanger an innocent person in the process," cried Cary angrily.

"What're you talking about?" If Jerico was faking the bewilderment with which he suddenly regarded her, Cary decided he was a better actor than she imagined possible. His reaction also made her feel rather silly. "I'm sorry I flew at you just then, Jerico. I'm a little tense." As she spoke, Cary studied him for a reaction—any reaction. Was Jerico more involved with the strange events taking place here than he admitted?

"You've felt evil here too, haven't you?" Jerico faced her, his dark intense eyes shining earnestly into hers. "It never used to be this way," he went on. "Only a year ago, everything was normal. Suddenly there's a whole new feeling about the place. I don't understand it, but it's here anyway."

Cary stared at him. For an instant, all her doubts about the boy melted. "Oh Jerico, you're right, and that's why I've been warning you about talking too much. I just don't feel it's safe. Like last night. That rug was intentionally untacked." Cary shuddered.

"You thought I did it, didn't you?" Jerico spoke calmly.

Cary bit her lip indecisively, then decided to be honest. "Yes, I did—you or Flora. I figured it had to be someone who slept downstairs because everybody else was upstairs and accounted for. Then I discovered the kitchen staircase. It comes out on the second floor. Now I don't know what to think."

Jerico took her hands as he gazed intently into her eyes. "I know I can't prove it, Cary," he said, "but I didn't do it. I wouldn't hurt you—not *you!* Please believe me." He clasped her face in his hands tightly—too tightly. His urgent strength hurt Cary.

"I believe you, Jerico." She just wanted him to let go. The vulnerable softness in his eyes had disappeared now and he was a stranger again—a hungry, desperate alien. Suddenly Cary thought she saw something in those eyes that wasn't there before. She felt suddenly afraid. Struggling free of his clasp, she ran away toward the house.

Chapter Fourteen

Back at the house, Cary found Janette, Marie and Flora unpacking huge bags of groceries in the kitchen. "Hello," she said, catching her breath, "May I help?"

"No, that's all right, dear." Janette gave her a grateful smile while Marie started to pour a five pound sack of flour into a painted tin canister. "It's a pity you woke so late," she continued. "We could have picked up some small things for you had we seen you before we left."

"Oh, you have a car?" Cary asked in some surprise. Somehow she had developed the impression that the household was self-contained in its isolation and needed neither traffic nor commerce with the surrounding populations.

"Oh, it's quite old, really, and doesn't run as well as it used to. Still, it gets us to Banting and back." She peered at Cary intently. "Why dear, is something wrong?" Her still sharp eyes caught hint of Cary's carefully concealed emotional turmoil.

"Oh nothing, really. I'm just feeling a little under." Cary didn't want to discuss her sudden fear of Jerico's presence —not just yet. She needed a chance to think things over. "Where's Charon?"

"Up in her room, I suppose." Marie's voice had a brittle edge as she answered Cary's question.

Flora, lazily stacking bright cans of ham, tuna, fruits and vegetables in the floor cupboard, ignored the young guest. Although Cary felt left out, she watched a few minutes then turned to head upstairs. "Don't be late for dinner," Janette called out behind. "We're having a roast tonight."

72

Passing down the hall to Charon's room, she stood before the girl's door and knocked. "Charon?" Cary called hesitantly because she didn't want to barge right in.

"It's open." Charon's voice sounded muffled as Cary pushed open the heavy door. Once inside, she saw her friend standing in front of the heavy, ornately carved, mirrored teakwood dresser. It had been pulled about three feet to the right and five feet away from its original resting spot. Charon's hands pressed tightly together. Although she panted from exertion, her large blue eyes snapped brightly from her pale, begrimed face in a triumphant glow. "I found it!" Charon's voice trembled in excitement.

"Found what?"

"How that awful creature got into my room, that's what I found!" Her eyes widened in wonder at the magnitude of her discovery. "Watch!"

She walked to a stretch of freshly exposed wall and pressed her hand against one particular flower in the busy pattern. Immediately, Cary heard a faint hissing which lasted for about five seconds. She gasped in surprise, for a portion of that wall began to move. It opened out into a low gaping passage cut against the floor. It hadn't shown there before. As it came into view, Charon shoved her heavy dressing table back into its customary place.

The vanity was the height of a low table, and extended about four feet across. Its top had been designed to hold perfume bottles, cosmetic jars, and all the other frou frou that ladies of its period were likely to set upon it. A matching teak mirror hung from the wall at the eye level of whomever sat before it. Three shallow drawers had been built on either side. The space between was completely hollow, without a backboard of any kind. Ordinarily wallpaper showed behind, but right now the space was a darkly gaping cavern.

"It's like something out of one of those terrible paperback novels I read." Cary stared in awe. "How did you ever discover it?"

"I'd heard stories about the manor's secret passages when I was a child. When I finally moved here I looked over the place rather casually and decided it was too solidly built for such nonsense. Today I looked again, more carefully. I knew I would've seen if that creature had entered and left

73

my room through the door or window, so I decided there had to be another access I hadn't noticed." Charon laughed aloud. "You should've seen me, Cary. I practically did a Sherlock Holmes with a magnifying glass. I concentrated on that area where she had seemed to disappear. After looking over the walls and everything, I decided to move the dresser. I didn't really expect anything to come of it, but well, I noticed that one flower—the one I showed you— seemed different. The petals, you see, are slightly mis- shapen and the color is darker. I touched it, and presto!"

"It's amazing." Cary crouched to get a better look into the space beyond. "Have you explored it?"

"I was waiting for you." Charon stared in half-fearful eagerness at her friend. "I was scared to go it alone, but with the two of us it ought to be safe enough."

Cary nodded silently, then stood. "We'll need a flash- light."

"I think there's one in the broom closet. I'll go look." Charon bustled out of her room. Cary spent the next few minutes, while her friend rummaged in the closet, staring into the darkness beyond. When Charon returned, slightly breathless and flushed, she clutched a battered tin light.

"Are the batteries any good?" Cary stared at the thing doubtfully.

"I checked already. It works."

Cary turned to the girl. "You first, or me?"

Charon paused, bit her lip, then glanced sheepishly at Cary. "If I give you the flashlight, will you go first?"

"I was afraid of that." Cary replied jokingly. "Yeah, I'll go."

She took the light, crouched at the mouth leading into the passage, then played its rounded beam on the threshold and beyond. To her surprise, the space opened into a narrow landing. A well defined set of carpeted steps led down from it. Directing the battery powered glare upward, she saw that the ceiling was high enough for them to stand. "How very interesting," she murmured. Cary crawled through, then stood, waiting for Charon. After her friend followed, the two crept down the narrow hidden stairway.

As they progressed deeper into the manor's dusty bowels, the beam bounced a circular pattern of shadows and light off the close, high walls. The illumination revealed a fine network of cracks in the plaster. Occasionally, there were large areas where it had fallen off completely. Someone had painted the walls, as far as Cary could tell in the semi-gloom, a grayish beige. Spider webs hung from the ceiling and there was the pervasive smell of mildew. "Charming!" Cary murmured drily as she stared around.

"Tradition has it that the original owner of the house built these passages so that he could invite special enemies down for hunts or fêtes. In the night, he'd sneak into their rooms through the secret entrances and kill them while they slept." Charon's voice sounded hollow and eerie in the gloom.

"The perfect host!" Cary observed sardonically.

"Kind of a Borgia, really, although he didn't seem to have used poison."

"You never know. He sounds like someone who'd use anything handy." Cary turned to Charon. "Did anyone tell you that you have one pip of a family tree?"

Charon laughed, then spoke seriously. "Yes, I suppose that's the whole problem, really." A stricken expression grew in her eyes.

"What is it?" Cary stared anxiously.

"Oh Cary, what if it's true? What if I've inherited the Parveau taint? Just because it's only a kind of mental illness doesn't make it any less terrifying. What if all the sickening evil that's been happening is because of me?"

Cary reached up to her friend's thin shoulders and shook them urgently. With burning eyes, she tried to bring Charon out of her sudden morbid mood. "Listen, there's something foul going on here, but it's not coming from you. It may be because of you, but if anything, you're the victim not the culprit. You weren't the one who untacked that carpet last night. I know that, because I was with you."

"I wasn't talking about that." Charon murmured faintly, her eyes averted. "I meant the dreams that seem to be real —where I'm outside wandering around—strange violent dreams. I wake up in a cold sweat and I'm never sure it didn't really happen."

"Nightmares are often that vivid, Charon." Cary tried to soothe the girl with sympathetic common sense.

"Mine are more than that." The girl replied grimly. "Once I even found mud caked to the bottom of my feet,

75

and I know I hadn't climbed into bed like that the night before."

"There's got to be a rational explanation." Cary spoke with dogged determination. "That can't happen by itself. Maybe you sleepwalk and you don't even know it. That could easily account for the muddy feet."

"Maybe so." Charon remained obviously unconvinced.

Both descended the steps silently until they came to a lower floor. "We're on the ground level, aren't we?" Charon stared around.

"Look for a door set into the wall. I want to see where we come out down here." Cary strained her eyes to peer through the darkness.

Suddenly Charon gasped. "Up ahead! I saw something moving." Before she finished speaking, Cary sprinted forward, her flashlight beaming a searching, rotating pattern. Charon followed close behind.

Neither of them noticed the sharp drop in the floor ahead. Before Cary even realized what happened, she was plummeting downward in darkness. "Charon!" She gasped her friend's name weakly. She was certain, however, from the moment she called out, that her warning would do no good.

The sandlike surface on which Cary landed, knees first, was sprinkled with random sharp edges of what she guessed to be gravel. Before she could even roll into a more comfortable position, she heard Charon's short, startled scream. She too had run off the edge and landed beside her friend.

"Charon, are you all right?" Cary grabbed the flashlight, which she had dropped, and played its beam against the five foot high wall over which they had just tumbled.

"Yes, a little startled is all." She stared after Cary at the drop. "I presume that was meant to be a booby trap. It was probably designed to sufficiently startle anyone not familiar with it, thereby giving my ancestor a chance to escape."

"Ingenious!" Cary replied with the faintest hint of sarcasm.

Charon shrugged. "It worked, didn't it?"

Cary stood and brushed herself clean. Suddenly their flashlight began to flicker. She turned to Charon. "Did you by any chance fall on this?"

"No. I'd have noticed if I had, though. It's pretty large and hard."

"We'd better head back," said Cary. "This light won't last too much longer the way it's flickering."

The two young women turned around. After pushing themselves up over the low wall, they hurried toward the stairway. Suddenly the light flickered out for good, leaving both in total darkness. Charon gasped in panic.

Chapter Fifteen

"Don't worry." Cary spoke soothingly. "There's only one way up, so we'll just grope our way back to the stairs and start climbing." Being around someone more fearful than she always seemed to bring out a bravery in Cary that otherwise didn't exist.

"I know it's silly, but I'm afraid." Charon's voice, emerging from the blackness behind Cary, trembled.

"I understand." Reaching back, Cary groped for Charon with outstretched arms. "Here, take my hand." When their fingers finally met, Cary grabbed Charon's tightly. Clutching at each other, they stumbled to the steps and safety.

Upon reaching the narrow flight, they started to climb. After twenty steps, the two girls came to a landing. They groped in three directions until they finally found the second staircase. It led up yet another twenty steps. "We should be close to your room by now." Cary tried to peer through the darkness for a faint glimmering of light, then turned to Charon. "You left the passage open so we could find it again—didn't you?" She heard a sharp, panic stricken intake of breath.

"Yes!" The girl's voice quavered. "Since we only went down two flights to get to the first floor, we should be right by my room. It shouldn't be this difficult." An edge of panic corroded the girl's ordinarily soft voice.

"It's all right." Cary spoke firmly, for she hoped to keep that from happening. "Maybe it slammed shut, or maybe we counted wrong."

"It seems to veer off this way." Charon tugged Cary's arm and guided her left.

"We should stick to the stairs," replied Cary. "We never left them before."

"You're right." When they found the third flight, they climbed upward, saying nothing to break the suddenly uneasy silence. Finally they reached yet another landing.

"Now what? I'm sure we've gone past it somehow. Maybe we turned off in a wrong direction."

Ahead, down a short corridor leading to the right, Cary spied the faint glimmering of light that shown there as a low crack between wall and floor. "Over there." She gasped in relief and lunged toward it. Charon, whom she still clutched by the wrist, dragged along behind.

Cary crouched to examine the spot. "It appears to be a hatch or door," she whispered. "I wonder where it leads."

"The more appropriate question," interjected Charon, "is how are we going to get it open and us out of here?"

"If it's not our room, it's probably a set-up just like it. We simply find the correct spot, push it, and the whole thing should give way."

Cary's fingers pressed and slid over the adjoining surface above and around the narrow, floor level crack. Suddenly her right hand hit upon a metallic protrusion. Pressing against it, she achieved no results. As she pulled her hand away however, her fingers accidentally touched another metallic object. It turned out to be a handle. She grabbed it eagerly and pulled. The panel immediately swung inward on silent hinges. Both young women crawled through the freshly exposed hatchway into an unfamiliar room.

Cary turned to Charon. "Where are we?"

"I don't know. I've never seen this room before. In fact, I didn't even know it existed."

"How very interesting." Cary examined their new surroundings.

The long, narrow and dim chamber's eaved ceiling betrayed its attic location, while the torrid Indian summer sun baked its stuffy air into suffocating heat. Cary walked quietly to the dusty window and looked out. Below, bathed in twilight purple, lay the soggy land of Charon's estate, and beyond, the black silent marsh. The room overlooked the land behind the manor.

Dusty antique furniture filled the room itself. The bed posters had been carved of a pale wood. The patina had mellowed with the years until its surface shown softly golden and felt as smooth as driftwood. Attached to the four high posters was a dusty canopy. It had been decorated with finely knotted pink lace that age had faded, dust had grayed and the relentless bayou humidity had streaked. Unknown hands had folded a matching coverlet and pillows set upon the mattress. "What a lovely old room!" Charon whispered in awed delight. "I wish I had known about it before. I'd love to use it as my own."

Just then, Cary heard the faint tread of approaching footsteps. "Ssshh! Someone's coming."

Charon glanced around urgently. "What should we do?"

Cary's mind whirred rapidly. Even though Charon owned the house, Cary suspected that their presence had best go undetected. She didn't want to put anyone on guard—not just yet. The steps grew louder as the unknown person shuffled closer to the door that had been cut into a wall on the opposite side of the room.

"Get back in that corridor and we'll spy on whoever it is." Cary grabbed Charon by her upper arm, shoved her through the opened porthole, then followed close behind. Once both were safe in the clandestine passage, Cary pulled the hatch almost closed. Only one tiny crack did she keep open to peer through.

From her hiding place Cary was able to see only a tantalizing glimpse of the room. She watched in fascination as the knob, which fell within her line of vision, turned. The door swung open.

Late afternoon sun had cast eerie shadows across the already dim little room as a pair of spindly legs stumbled through the opening. The legs moved forward stealthily, into the room's center as their owner began to potter about. Cary heard her pull open one drawer after another, shuffle through the papers inside, then slam each shut. Even though Cary's hiding spot restricted her view to one tiny area, she was sure she knew to whom those legs belonged.

Just then the intruder bent to inspect inside a pillowcase that had been placed upon the bed, and Cary was able to confirm her guess. For there, backlit by the long mellow beams of late afternoon sun she saw the flaccid profile of the sisters' alcoholic live-in housekeeper Flora.

The two young women arrived at the dinner table dusty and breathless. "You're late." Marie glanced at Charon with questioning stare. "I'm afraid your meat mightn't be as rare as you like. I'll tell Janette you're here though. She's cooking tonight."

"I take it that Flora's indisposed?" Charon spoke with half humorous irony, knowing perfectly well why Flora hadn't been around to cook dinner.

Marie sighed. "I really have no idea where she is. I'm afraid that woman's getting to be more trouble than she's worth." Marie shook her head then turned distractedly toward the kitchen. "I'd better help Janette."

After she had left, Cary turned to Charon. "What did she mean, your meat not being as rare as you like? You always took it extra well done." More than once, when the two had dined out together at a popular steak house near their campus, Cary's own dinner had been delayed an extra five or ten minutes because of Charon's insistance on over-cooked meat.

"Not anymore, I don't," retorted her friend. "My tastes have changed." Their conversation stopped when Janette carried a steaming roast into the dining room. At the edge of the platter had been set a chunk wrapped in foil.

"I cut off a section for you, dear," she said, smiling at Charon. "I wrapped it in tin foil when I realized you'd be late. I hope it's still warm."

"It'll be fine." Charon spoke reassuringly. She reached for her own piece of underdone roast. After setting it on her plate she unwrapped and crumpled the dripping foil into a ball. When the girl cut into the browned chunk, Cary saw with surprise that the bright red meat inside gushed with blood.

"Isn't that just a little too underdone?" She ventured to ask the question tactfully.

"Maybe a shade so." Charon replied imperturbably as she closed her mouth over a dainty sized chunk. "Anyway, I told you my tastes have changed."

Cary didn't bother to reply as her attention focused on her own dinner. Marie passed her a plate piled high with corn, mashed potatoes and generous slices of lightly pink, medium rare and thoroughly tender prime roast.

Chapter Sixteen

Eight hours later in the dead of night, Cary woke to the sound of one lone drum. It beat a forlorn tattoo against the darkness. Alarmed, she propped herself on one elbow and strained to listen. The noise seemed to come from outside. It wafted in through her open window. Throwing her sheet back, Cary slid out of her bed and crept across the room. She peered out into the moonlit yard but saw nothing. After stepping over the threshold onto her balcony, she strained to catch a glimpse of the unseen activity. Even there, however, the mysterious drummer played his solo out of her view. The noise, seeming to grow louder now, pulsed from behind the solid brick mansion.

Tantalized, she slid a robe over her nightgown and stealthily cracked her door. She peered out. When she saw that the darkness beyond seemed deserted, Cary slipped out into the hall. She pulled the door shut silently and hurried down the stairs. Reaching the front door, she tried to open it. To her dismay, however, it refused to give. She groped in the darkness for the lock but found the inside key removed. With chilling realization, she knew that someone had purposely locked her inside.

But Cary wasn't one to give up so easily. After trying the kitchen door and finding that it too had been sealed, she went into the parlor. One window overlooked a thick mass of dark green foundation shrubbery. She reached to unfasten the simple sliding lock, then pushed up the bottom sash. To her intense delight, the wood framed glass panel gave way with noiseless ease. As it opened, Cary heard the drum's throbbing more clearly. It seemed louder now, and had been joined by hoarse voices raised in chanting.

Cary swung her feet over the ledge, letting them hang, then slid until her toes almost reached the bushes below. She let herself drop. The shrubbery rustled and crackled with a burst of soft sound as she landed. Its lacy needled foliage scratched Cary's bare legs. A nightgown, she decided, was decidedly impractical for sneaking around in the dead of night. Outside, the drum beat seemed to come from everywhere. After disentangling herself, Cary crept toward the direction from which it sounded strongest. Her heart pounded wildly in time to its noise as she reached the edge of the house. There, the wall turned in a forty-five degree angle and became another wall.

From her hiding place against its bricks, Cary peered out toward the grounds. Again she saw nothing. The sound definitely came from the rear.

She hurried toward it through the damp grass. When she reached the wall's end she pressed herself between the bushes that grew against the foundation. Using them as cover, she glanced around the corner to the land that stretched from the house's rear to the trees hiding the mausoleum beyond. Cary gasped in shocked surprise, then stared—unable to really believe what she saw.

She kneeled to creep closer. As her knees sank into the slimy mud earth, Cary focused her attention on the bizarre scene taking place under the cold light of a full moon. On the dew covered grass had been built a bonfire. Through its transparent flames she could see faces. Cary's eyes riveted upon them. She crept as near as she dared to that fire. Concealed by shadows, crouched on her haunches and bent almost double, she stared as a tongue of flame leapt upward.

Its flickering candescence brought back to her the words of her old friend Victoria Lambeau—a brilliant young exchange student from Jamaica she had known in college. As the flame grew brighter, to become the echo of a thousand other fires, the image of Victoria's beautiful black face formed in her mind. Candle flame, bonfire, funeral pyre, holocaust—the fire she watched now in hypnotized fascination brought with it the association of all fire. Victoria had spoken of such things late at night when the lights had been turned low. She had described faces—black and brown—

of people dressed in brightly colored rags crouching around piles of burning wood. Hidden high in the island mountains, they performed forbidden rites.

As Cary watched, a tall, gaunt woman swayed over the flames, leaning into them. Her crackling contralto voice wailed an invocation to Baron Samedi—the bringer of death. Marie, dressed in black shroudlike robes, chanted while soft voices hummed in harmony around her.

Cary gazed at the entranced faces as they stared mindlessly into the flames. Janette was there, and Flora. She stared at Flora with genuine surprise for within the span of a few hours the woman had transformed from a squinting drunkard into a fiery priestess of the Great God Voodoo.

Her gown was a winding sheet of black. Tied around her waist from a twisted silken cord hung the drum that had awakened Cary. She beat at its taut leather skin with ritualistic fervor. Its pulsing sound marked the time by which Janette and Marie chanted. The drone of the priestesses grew louder and shriller.

Janette careened toward the fire while the others glided in procession to surround her. The woman's plump body swayed in time to the chanting as she lifted high a writhing snake. Whipping furiously in a futile fight for freedom, it seemed to glow in the pyre's flickering light. Finally Janette lowered the creature to her shoulders then wrapped it around one arm.

As Cary watched out of sight in the shadows, the air crackled with primal nerve beats. Screams of ecstatic passion rent the air. Electrical vibe-waves paralyzed the breathless bayou night.

Their black clad bodies writhed as they called out again to Baron Samedi and the snake god Voodoo. Cary herself almost expected to see Baron Samedi's shadowy form, clad in ragged tails and top hat, emerge from the flames. Victoria had told her all about the death god.

Lips possessed by the Power, chanted praises in a long forgotten African tongue. Marie and Janette, partial descendants of slaves, wisely placated the ancient master of darkness.

Cary understood. Her friend Victoria, an educated young black woman from those islands had feared Baron

Samedi too. But then, reflected Cary, what is Baron Samedi but another name for death, and who isn't afraid of dying?

Around the fire, the three dancers grew more frenzied. Possessed women whirled, their backs bent and their arms raised in supplication. They seemed to have forgotten their own identities. Cary smelled the sweat, felt the presence of The One as the heavily scented night air grew older.

Suddenly she heard the sound of someone walking. Feeling a pang of thrilled fascination, Cary listened as the weight of each foot—one after the other, bearing down in the wet grass—slushed closer. Her heart pounded violently. It seemed to erupt into the middle of her throat and choke her. She wanted to gasp for breath yet didn't dare for the noise would betray her presence to the dancers and whomever roamed close by. Her eyes darted as she cast about for escape.

The unseen being moved implacably forward. Only the bushes, thick and dark, seemed fit to shield her, so Cary crouched back into them and waited. The unknown person emerged around the corner into Cary's view. In fear she shrank closer against the wall. She hardly felt the prickling foliage scratch her.

At first, she saw only the silhouette of a man as he passed into view. As he stepped out of the shadows, into the moon's soft glow, Cary recognized the face of Marie's brooding young nephew. As he passed her, she saw his eyes fixed straight ahead and staring. He noticed neither Cary hidden in the bushes, nor even the bizarre ritual taking place on the lawn. He seemed to be in a world of his own making.

From those bushes, Cary watched Jerico tread slowly across the grass. When he disappeared into the shadows under a distant stand of trees, she stood and pulled herself free.

She wondered where he was going and what he knew. How could she account for his strange, trancelike behavior? With a shudder Cary considered the possibility that the loup-garou of the villagers' nightmares was more than merely superstition—that such a depraved, tormented creature actually existed as a human with a morbid craving for blood and flesh. It would be an angry, troubled person like

Jerico, she thought. Suddenly the flesh at the back of her neck creeped icily toward her scalp. In horror, Cary stared into the inky shadows through which the troubled youth had disappeared.

Chapter Seventeen

Early the following morning, the telephone rang. Shortly thereafter, Cary heard a knocking on her closed door. "Yes?" she called.

"Telephone fer yew, Miss Cary." She recognized Flora's nasal, twanging voice.

"I'll be right down." A strangely uneasy feeling gripped her now because the previous night's arcane rite had deeply impressed Cary.

More disconcerting had been the way all three women disappeared during Jerico's passing. What had become of them? She threw her bathrobe on over her torn and stained nightgown and hurried, still barefoot, downstairs.

By the time she picked up the receiver, Cary was panting breathlessly.

"Miss Matthews, is that you?" Young Dr. Gautier's anxious voice sounded over the line.

"What is it?" Something in his tone made her throat clutch.

"Another child is missing from Fleur-de-Lis." His words sounded flat and empty, as if they sprang from a weariness too deep to be expressed.

"Oh no!" Sweat sprang to the palms of Cary's hands. "How many does that make?"

"Six." His tone was reverent with horror.

"What're we going to do?"

"They're blaming you—that is, St. Anne Manor and its open."

you should leave. The town's about ready to blow wide inhabitants. There's some ugly talk going around. I think

"I can't," she replied. "Not just yet. Not until I can take Charon with me. Anyway, things are beginning to come out into the open." Speaking softly and rapidly with hand cupped against the phone's mouthpiece, she told him of the previous night's events. When she finished, the young doctor failed to reply. "Well?" Cary couldn't stand the silence.

"I don't think you should have told me all this over the phone. There may be an extension somewhere you don't know about. Anyway, the operator might be able to listen in."

"Is that all you have to say?" Cary wanted reassurance, sympathy and promise of aid, not a scolding.

Silence followed her question. Finally he spoke. "I don't like it."

"Well, neither do I, but I'm in it pretty deep now."

"Too deep. My invitation still holds. Call me if ever you need help and I'll come as soon as humanly possible. I'm on my way to deliver a baby now, but I've left instructions with my mother. If I'm not here, she'll know where to reach me."

"Thanks." After hanging up, Cary wandered into the kitchen. Jerico sat at the table. As she watched him drink a cup of the thick, black chicory coffee she had yet to grow used to, Cary decided to confront the boy with the news. "There's been another kidnapping from Fleur-de-Lis." In spite of herself, she stared at him almost accusingly. She couldn't forget his entranced face as he wandered last night toward the marsh.

Jerico shrugged. "I knew that hours ago." He bit into a piece of buttered toast.

"What do you mean?" That hadn't actually been the reaction Cary had hoped for.

"You late sleepers are the last to know everything. I've been up since six this morning." The youth looked suitably smug at this announcement.

Cary wondered if the kid ever slept. Perhaps, she thought, that explained the dark circles always under his eyes.

"Yes indeed, Dear Lady, while you dozed in lovely slumber I paddled into Pecan Lagoon—a paradise you've never seen. Heard the news from Mack Latour, a hunter of my acquaintance. Word gets around quickly in these parts." When he spoke to Cary, his tone of voice seemed cold and hard. She guessed that his sudden aloofness had been caused by injured feelings when she had wrenched herself away from him the previous afternoon. She decided to make up to him, sensing it would not be wise to incur his enmity. Unless he was actually the one responsible for her mishaps, she decided he'd be more useful as her friend. Furthermore, her innate sense of fair play forbade Cary to condemn the boy without decent proof. "About yesterday." She sat in the chair facing him. "I didn't mean to run away like I did. It's just that I've been so nervous with all that's happened." She shrugged, making her face into a suitably abashed expression. "Suddenly I just got an attack of, well, *paranoia*, I guess." She smiled timidly at him.

Jerico shrugged. "I guess I had it coming, but I'm really sorry you thought I'd hurt you."

"As I said, I've been under a strain."

She wanted to ask Jerico why he had wandered outside last night. She reflected, however, that he in turn would have a perfect right to ask her the same question. Since she wasn't ready to explain her actions, or even let them be known, Cary let the whole matter drop.

"I'm really glad we're friends again." To her mild annoyance, Jerico now stared at her with the same longing expression in his eyes that she had noticed earlier, but she managed to depart gracefully and without incident.

All that day, during times when she encountered the sisters and Flora performing their mundane chores, Cary found it almost impossible to act natural. She watched Janette, clad in a crisp flowered house dress, do housework. In her mind she saw another Janette—the entranced priestess of Voodoo dancing before a crackling fire while a snake slithered around her pudgy upper arm.

As Flora stumbled about, obviously already under the influence of alcohol, a chill trickled up Cary's spine. Was she really all that intoxicated, or might it be an act she performed to avert suspicion from herself? Cary wished she knew. Flora of the daylight hours stumbled about and squinted as if she saw double. Flora of the night before had chanted to her alien god in a voice clear and strong.

Her body had swayed, not from the influence of corn mash liquor, but under the spell of a Dionysian ecstasy. Where was that Flora now? Seeing both of them, smiling and guileless, touched Cary with a fear that was cold and nasty.

She didn't feel the same about Marie. Marie gliding around a ceremonial pyre seemed consistent with the tall gaunt woman who glowered about the manor during daylight. Cary had always been a little afraid of Marie anyway.

That night, Cary didn't go to sleep, but paced in her room with the lights out as she waited for something to happen. Although she didn't know what to expect, or why, the feeling of unexplained dread that had grown familiar lately, warned her of impending danger.

She walked to her balcony and stood silently in the torpid, thickly humid night. The thin cotton gown that flowed from her shoulders billowed in the warm breeze that blew in off the marsh. An hour passed until the hands of her watch pointed to eleven.

She had waited, but nothing happened and now Cary grew restless. She couldn't sleep. She was tired of pacing the floor, and she knew she wouldn't be able to concentrate if she tried to read. Slipping on a pair of sandals, Cary left her room. She was sick of the house, its silence, and the mood of oppressive evil that pervaded its walls. She wanted to be outside where the air, if not fresh, was at least untainted.

She hurried through the parlor to the dining room and out the kitchen door. As it opened freely, Cary murmured half sarcastically as she passed outside. "What, no more voodoo parties?"

Under the waning moon the land lay serene. Crickets chirped and from far off she heard birds. All the usual noises of nocturnal marsh creatures wafted to her ears yet the effect was one of profound silence. Strange, she thought, how the noises people make are so much more obtrusive.

She wandered to the edge where reeds grew in the shallows. Keeping to the grass, she skirted the manor's estate, staring with dreamlike serenity into the lushly tangled growth now hidden by a mantle of darkness.

Suddenly, up ahead, she saw the white clad figure of a small child. Walking toward her, it stared past with unseeing eyes. "The missing child from Fleur-de-Lis!" She cried out and hurried toward the little creature, intending to embrace and guide it back to the manor. "It's lost." After feeding it, she would call Dr. Gautier and let him return the child to its parents. "It's all right, you're safe now." As she murmured words of comfort, Cary bent down to clasp the wandering tyke in her arms.

But the child, a little boy, shoved her away with such violent force that Cary catapulted backwards to land sprawled in the grass. All the while, the empty, strangely soulless expression in his eyes never changed. He passed her without seeming to notice what he had done as he glided along the marsh's edge toward the darkness beyond.

Cary stumbled to her feet and lunged forward, only to be stopped suddenly as a strong arm from behind grabbed around her waist. Cary cried out in horrified fear.

"Don't follow!" Jerico's voice sounded from behind, strangely hollow.

"Let me go!" Cary struggled to break free. "I can't let that child wander all alone like that. Something may happen to it."

"Something's already happened to it. That child's dead."

A sudden chill passed through Cary's flesh. "You're talking nonsense!" She forced herself to speak scornfully, to hide the withering fear that grew inside. "Dead children don't walk. Now let me go, I say!"

"I can't. He'll only hurt you. You felt his strength, didn't you, when he shoved you down? I saw that."

"He's a child. A sick, lost child who needs help!" Cary tried biting Jerico's arm, but couldn't reach it with her teeth. She kicked, but he knew when to pull his legs from reach. "Please let me go, Jerico." Her tone was pleading now, as she watched the little boy melt into the shadows.

"I told you," he said, "that child is already dead. He's a walking corpse. Didn't you see his eyes?"

Cary remembered those empty cold eyes with a shudder of horror. Memories of her Jamaican friend returned to her consciousness. Victoria had spoken, in hushed whispers, of the zombi—eternal slaves lost to Heaven and Hell. She was a Christian, and had been too well-educated to believe in the old superstitions until the summer of her sixteenth year. She had traveled with her father to a plantation hidden high in the island mountains—far away from the city and police. There she saw with her own eyes, she said, blank-eyed, heavy-limbed battalions trudging clumsily ahead as they labored in the rocky fields. They had needed neither food nor drink and had obeyed any command without question. Their strength, she had said, was phenomenal. From that summer on, Victoria had believed in the walking dead.

If that poor child was indeed a zombi, then those three old women practiced a rite more obscene than Cary believed possible. The night whirled and dimmed until Cary collapsed unconscious into Jerico's arms.

When she had awakened, Jerico had disappeared. She lay alone in the damp grass staring up at the stars and pallid moon. Her head rolled to the left as she tried to escape the horrible pounding inside it. Instead, the pounding seemed to grow louder. Groaning, Cary sat up, brushed the dew off her arms and gown, then stumbled groggily to her feet.

The rhythmic beating continued and Cary realized with a sudden clutch of horror, that the sound was not within her head, but outside. On the rolling lawn behind the house another voodoo rite was taking place!

She stumbled toward the manor, her knees weak with horror. Creeping closer, she concealed herself in the shadows and watched. In order to see more clearly, Cary crawled yet closer, to the very edge of the concealing darkness.

Overhead, a waning moon beamed down a dim cold light. In the same spot had been built another ritual pyre. Through its transparent flames flickered faces.

No, Cary thought excitedly to herself, it isn't the same! Instead of three worshippers stood four.

Cary's eyes riveted upon the young woman who stood entranced behind the glowing conflagration. Charon, with eyes closed and hair streaming about her pale face, waited passively as three eerily shrouded forms glided around her and the fire. Charon's long white night gown and flowing pale hair combined with her increasing emaciation to accent the girl's almost spectral beauty. Her hands hung limply at her sides as she swayed. What was Charon doing at a voodoo rite? Questions and doubts flooded Cary's mind.

She stared in fascination as the three veiled creatures closed in. Through the black transparent shrouds covering their faces, Cary recognized the three old women. Both Janette and Flora writhed in a state of advanced frenzy around the girl. Only Marie seemed to be in control of herself. She glided over to a tiny white kid that had been tethered to a stake jutting out of the ground. The shadows flickering over its body created an aura of unreality around the little creature. Only its eyes, black and frightened, seemed alive. It bleated piteously as Marie untied the knot looped around the wood. The chanting around Charon grew louder.

Marie, apparently acting as high priestess this night, led the little animal toward the flames—toward Charon. Reaching to the entranced girl, Marie placed the rope against Charon's palm, then folded her fingers around it. When she seemed satisfied that Charon had grasped it securely, Marie stepped away. The chanting and drumbeats pounded faster.

Both Janette and Marie helped Charon to kneel. They eased her around until she faced the kid, her eyes fixed on its own. Still clutching the tether, Charon waited. Though her own eyes shown as frightened as the little animal's, she didn't move, but instead stared in horrified fascination as Marie raised a huge knife high over it.

Suddenly Charon came to herself. "No!" She cried out in horror, leaped to her feet and reached to stay Marie's arm. "I can't go through with it. I won't let you kill an innocent animal as a blood sacrifice! I'm not worth it—not anymore." As the girl burst into convulsive sobbing, she whirled and ran toward the house. Cary, still crouched in hiding, breathed a sigh of relief and watched as Marie led the goat away from the fire. As the ritual that followed among the three took on the same form as the night before, Cary backed away to return inside.

Chapter Eighteen

The following morning dawned gray and brooding. Summer's final fling before autumn was over. Although the leaves remaining on the trees kept their green color, the cold morning air hit Cary's face as she rolled over and opened her eyes.

She lay in bed, content to remain in warmth. Thinking of the deep bruises where Jerico had grabbed her, Cary flinched. They hurt, and the ones on her legs where she had landed knee first in the wet grass seemed raised and swollen. Her entire body ached from the cold and damp.

She had sneaked back into the house through the unlocked kitchen door, following close behind Charon who never noticed. She had fallen into bed wearily as dawn streaked purple across the eastern sky. The clock on her bed now read ten o'clock.

"Oh, well," she murmured, "that's five or six hours sleep anyway." After half an hour, Cary stepped out of bed then started to dress. She hoped to inspect the fire site without anyone knowing what she was up to. Perhaps she might even find signs of that strange child as well. She hurried silently downstairs, her fingertips lightly touching the dull mahogany bannister.

Sweeping out toward the kitchen and the rear door, Cary stopped short. Just as she was about to leave the house, Jerico, bursting through the white painted basement door, startled her. She flinched in surprise. "Oh, you scared me."

"You're getting jumpy," he said with a grin. "Next you'll start disintegrating like your friend." Cary noticed that the deep circles under his eyes seemed darker than before. He stared at her almost accusingly. "You look tired."

A faint tremor gripped Cary as she wondered whether he knew about the voodoo rites his aunt, Janette and Flora practiced.

"I'm not tired." She spoke with a nonchalant shrug. Neither of them mentioned the wandering child.

"Then why do you have circles under your eyes?" Jerico cocked his head and lifted one eyebrow. Cary said nothing as she returned his stare with a look of studied innocence.

"I'm coming down with a cold," she finally replied. She stared at him boldly. "I'm afraid sleeping out on the lawn has a way of disagreeing with me. I always catch a cold."

Jerico glanced up. "After you fainted, I went after your baby zombi."

"And?"

Jerico shrugged. "He was gone."

Cary regarded him intently. "How do you suppose he came to be that way—assuming that he's actually a zombi and not just a sick, lost child?"

Jerico scowled, remaining silent for a second, then peered at her slyly. "You've been up and creeping around outside. You must've seen things. What do you think?"

Cary wondered how much Jerico actually knew. How much of what he said was only bluff? Any further speculation was cut short, however, by the pale, wan young woman who joined them in the kitchen. Seeing her, Jerico grinned sardonically. "We all seem to have circles under our eyes this morning." He made the remark pointedly, as if he too had witnessed the strange ritual sacrifice that had almost taken place in the night. Cary wondered if he knew what had become of the frightened baby goat.

"I'll leave you two in peace. I'm sure you have much to discuss." After Jerico left them alone, Charon shivered.

"He frightens me," she whispered.

"Charon, what were you doing outside last night?" Cary had wanted to restrain herself from asking that question but curiosity overwhelmed her. Charon's eyes widened in guilty fear. "How—how did you know?" As her voice trembled, Cary felt a pang of regret for bringing the subject up.

"I couldn't sleep last night so I went outside, hoping for

96

a good walk would tire me out. When I heard the drum-beat, I went to find out what was happening."

"And you saw it all." Charon averted her eyes. "It might've been dangerous for you. I don't mean because of us, but the loup-garou—it might've been roaming." Charon shuddered. "But then again," she added softly, "it probably wasn't." The girl raised her eyes in despair and Cary understood her thoughts.

"You're not that." Cary spoke briskly, feeling herself to represent the Voice Of Reason. "You are, however, a silly idiot for standing around in that cold, wet grass in the dead of night and letting three old women perform an absurd ritual around you. You could've caught pneumonia. What was all that nonsense about, anyway?"

"It wasn't nonsense." Charon replied curtly. "The women practice Obeah—a religion as old as Africa. Marie and Janette learned those rites from their mother, and they were trying to help me overcome—" Charon trailed off wistfully. "But I couldn't let them go through with it. Fighting blood with blood frightened me." The young woman withdrew into herself while Cary stared in disbelief. Charon, of all people, consenting to what years ago she would have called 'superstition'. Was this yet another sign of her deterioration? Cary's mind whirled with unanswered questions. Were all three women responsible for her voodoo death threat and murder attempt or only one? And that child—could such things as zombis actually exist? She could almost believe in them as she listened to Victoria back at school, for the young woman's glowing black eyes and hushed contralto voice had woven a spell. But what Victoria had claimed to see existed in Jamaica and Haiti. On those dark islands anything was possible, but the idea that zombis walked here in the United States—Cary suppressed a shudder.

Feeling a surge of panic, she took a deep breath and forced herself to remain calm. "But I had always imagined that those women were Christian." She stared into Charon's eyes. "I'm sure I've seen Marie wear a little silver cross. Is that just to mislead?"

Charon shook her head as she too grew calmer. "No, Marie believes in Christianity too. They all do. The two religions, old and new, co-exist peacefully in both Janette

97

and Flora. In Marie, they rage a battle to tear her apart. The commandment 'Thou shalt have no other gods before me' frightens her." Charon started toward the back door. "I'll see you later." For the first time, Cary noticed that her friend had dressed to go out.

"Where are you going?"

"I'll let you know later." Charon replied mysteriously. "I've some business to attend to in Banting."

As her friend hurried out of view toward the garage, Cary stared after her in bewilderment. What did Charon need in Banting, and why was she being so secretive? The young woman stood quietly to collect her disarrayed thoughts.

She decided to spend the rest of the morning in her room with a good book. The weather was too bleak for her to wander outside, and even if the cloud covered sun could warm the chill air, she felt too tired to do anything strenuous anyway. Cary turned and hurried upstairs.

Upon seeing her closed door, she felt mildly surprised. She distinctly remembered leaving it open earlier. Grabbing the knob, she yanked it.

Revealed through the opening door stood Flora bent over the open top drawer of her desk. She was so absorbed in the task of rifling through Cary's box of personal letters that she failed to notice when Cary herself entered the room. At the girl's outraged yelp of righteous indignation, however, the woman whirled with a furtively guilty expression fixed on her face. "Just what are you doing?" Cary strode forward and grabbed the box from the woman's hand.

Flora smiled shiftily. "Jest cleanin' up, Miss," she said, then shuffled toward Cary's door. "Jest cleanin' up."

As she made her escape down the hall, her wedgies clunking on the floor, Cary stared after in outraged disbelief.

Chapter Nineteen

Throughout the waning afternoon, the clouds gathered thick and dark overhead. The air crackled with electricity and humidity grew denser. Janette, who stood at the sink preparing crayfish for the night's supper, glanced out the window as Cary wandered aimlessly into the kitchen.

"Storm's brewing." She announced the obvious in her typically pleasant manner. Only now, with the memory of moonlit rites fresh in her mind, Cary searched for sinister undercurrents. There seemed to be none in Janette, which made it all the more horrible. Even as she stared apprehensively at the old woman, however, Cary's innate sense of justice reminded her that Janette's flirtation with voodoo was probably entirely innocent—nothing more than a mild thrill for an elderly, bored spinster. In daylight, she felt rather silly for believing Jerico's wild stories about the child being a zombi. She decided to carry on as usual by voicing a complaint about Flora. "I must have a word with you about that woman."

"You mean Flora?" Janette clicked her tongue sadly. "Strange, how everybody uses that same tone of voice when they want to discuss Flora. What exactly did she do now?"

Cary stared dumbfounded. Could she be talking about the same woman she had danced with in such abandon the night before? "I caught her snooping in my private letters," she answered aloud.

Janette frowned. "That's her worst fault—next to her drinking. Someday that woman's long nose will get her into serious trouble. The next time you catch her, be as mean as you like. She needs to be taught a lesson."

The priestess of the god Voodoo had been replaced by the simple, anxious old woman Cary had thought she knew so well. The transformation confused her. What should she believe? For the time being, however, she let herself be lulled. Always feeling afraid, suspicious of everyone was too horrible a way to live. She could have called Dr. Gautier, talked matters over with him and thereby eased her own mind, but pride kept Cary from doing so. She didn't want to burden him any more than necessary.

That night, a clap of thunder booming close by woke her. Cary opened her eyes and blinked. Still groggy, she only knew that she had lost the thread of an extremely interesting dream. The room, pitched in deep darkness, brightened harshly as a lightening bolt ripped across the sky outside her window. Its illumination backlit the raindrops that beaded the windowglass.

Cary, who loved a good thunderstorm, sat up and then swung her feet onto the floor. She decided to capture it, if possible, on paper. Walking to the desk, she pulled out her sketchbook and a thick leaded drawing pencil. As she passed the heater vent however, Cary stopped suddenly. Sniffing the air, she stared in horror at its innocuous grid covered opening. Unlit gas, pouring through it with a soft but constant hiss, assailed her nostrils with its pungent odor.

Cary, her face icy as much from fear now as from cold, hurried to her double window and tried to throw it open. She failed. Someone had locked it. Crying out in shocked surprise, she hurried to her door. As the stink of gas grew heavier in the air, she tried to escape into the relative safety of the hall.

Cary rattled the knob. She tried to coax it into yielding but failed. As the implacable hiss from behind grew louder in her frightened imagination, Cary stifled a sob and rushed again to the window. To break the glass and breathe fresh air was her only chance, for the poisonous fumes had already entered her bloodstream. Her head grew heavy and her mind groggy.

She trembled as she searched in pitch darkness for something with which to batter the window. She found nothing. Nearly overcome, Cary lifted one bent elbow and jabbed it against the unyielding glass. She thrust at it again and again, battering until the pane finally cracked. Shards tinkled and crackled to the floor.

Cary pressed her face against the jagged opening, breathing deeply as fresh night air poured through. After a few minutes, she was able to kick out the lower pane. She shattered the flimsy wood dividers as well as the glass itself and thus accomplished an escape. Forcing her body through the narrow opening, she collapsed into a dead faint on the rainsoaked balcony.

Janette discovered Cary the following morning. She opened the girl's now unlocked bedroom door. Upon peering inside, she had seen Cary's body through the broken glass and screamed. Marie came running at the sound, following her half sister into the room. "Why, Miss Cary!" Janette gasped as she stared in horror at the young woman's scratched face and arms. Her flesh, from breaking through the jagged glass to safety, had been nastily scratched.

Cary opened her eyes and stared groggily. Suddenly she figured out where she was and why. "Oh no! Someone tried to kill me."

"Why, whatever are you talking about?" Marie frowned.

"Someone turned on the gas in my room. Just the gas and no flame. When the thunder woke me up, I smelled it. I tried to get out, but my window and door was locked."

"But my dear," Janette retorted mildly, "how do you think I got into your room?"

Cary's eyes widened. "But it was locked last night, I tell you. I tried, but I couldn't open it."

"Perhaps the dampness made something swell." Her patronizing tone irritated Cary. It was as if the old woman was trying to humor her.

"I tell you I tried the knob and pulled as hard as I could, but it wouldn't open. I was nearly unconscious."

"You were certainly lucky to wake up," said Janette. Marie, standing behind, glared silently at the damaged window. Cary felt the unpleasant suspicion that Marie was more concerned with the mess than over her narrow escape from death. "It was horrible!" Cary stared at the old woman pleadingly, as if asking forgiveness for the necessity of saving her own life at the expense of the broken window.

"I'm sure it was." The old woman spoke grimly as she turned to leave.

"I don't think she likes me." Cary stared ruefully at Janette.

"Oh, don't mind Marie." She gave Cary a warm smile. "It's just her way."

Suddenly they were interrupted by a scream from the kitchen. "That was Marie!" Cary stumbled to her feet.

"I do believe you're right," cried Janette. She bustled toward the stairway. Cary followed as best she could, but her head still reeled from the effects of the gas, loss of blood and excitement.

"Janette!" Marie's anguished cry sent both scurrying faster toward the kitchen.

"We're coming." Janette's breathless voice gasped in reply as her feet touched the ground floor and hurried toward her sister. When she reached the kitchen, she too screamed. Cary, catching up, stared through the doorway into the scene that Marie had discovered.

Blood everywhere. Blood splattered on the white enamel painted cupboards. Blood had discolored the oil cloth covered kitchen table. Blood had even congealed in puddles on the linoleum floor. In one such puddle, Flora's dirty black wedgie rested on its side. "Where's Flora?" Janette stared at the scene with wide, horrified eyes.

"I don't know." Marie, with a quietly grim set to her features, studied the stains.

Cary gazed in horrified fascination. "For that matter, where's Charon?"

"Why, I don't know." Janette frowned in sudden puzzlement, while Marie glanced around.

"I'm surprised all the screaming didn't arouse her," said Marie.

"I'll go see if she's all right." Cary, still a little dizzy, careened toward the stairway. Clutching onto the bannister, she stumbled upward.

Knocking on Charon's door, she received no answer. After finding it unlocked, she stepped inside. The first thing Cary saw was that Charon's bed had not been slept in. Every piece of furniture, every ornament was exactly where it should be. The double windows, leading out onto Charon's balcony, however, swayed unlatched. Through them poured cold but damp autumn air.

"Charon?" Cary hurried toward the open window. "Charon!" The balcony too was empty. As she passed the mirrored dressing table, her eyes fixed on the space underneath. Only busy wallpaper showed there now, as if the strange passage behind had never existed.

She felt an urgent necessity to find her friend. It was as if some primal instinct she could never hope to understand sensed the girl was in trouble. Somehow her mind had linked that dead-eyed child with Charon—as if deep inside she sensed they both shared a common fate.

A chill rippled Cary's flesh as she wondered by what means did the girl's unknown enemy mean to accomplish her death. And if an attempt did indeed meet with success and Charon died, Cary feared she'd then be robbed not only of her life, but of her soul as well. Suddenly the idea of zombis seemed more gruesomely real than ever before.

She ran downstairs and burst outdoors. There, Cary felt safe even though she knew the enemy could still stalk her. Her instincts however sensed differently. Any evil that existed here lay within the old house itself. Fear lurked in those corridors and something alien lived within the rotten catacombs buried in the walls. Outdoors, however, all smelt clean, sweet and wholesome, and Cary felt relieved to be there.

She wandered into the thicket of cypress behind the house. Standing among them, she looked up, admiring for a brief moment the beauty she saw there. Suddenly Cary heard a rustling behind her. Whirling, she searched for its source then gasped in horror. Lying half buried in the mud was Charon. Her hair was tangled, her eyes vacant. Her hand clutched a black object.

"Charon!" Cary gasped as she hurried to the girl's side. She knelt down just as Charon drew her hand away from the black thing. As she did, Cary recognized Flora's other shoe. It rested on its side in the muddy soil. "Charon, what happened?" Cary helped the girl into a sitting position.

"I—I don't know." As she whispered, the girl clasped her face with one hand. "I just woke up."

"Charon, there's something you must try to remember." Cary became very serious. "How did you get hold of this?"

She lifted Flora's scuffed wedgie and handed it to her friend. The dazed girl took it, stared at it in bewilderment then handed it back. "I—I don't know," she murmured, shaking her head. "It was just there when I started waking."

"Try to remember!" Cary gripped Charon's shoulder and squeezed it gently. "It's important. Are you sure you can't think of anything? Perhaps a memory—some association?"

Charon frowned in doubt as she bit her lip. "No," she said, and sighed. "I don't know." Her voice grew almost angry.

Cary reached for Charon's arm. "Here, let me help you up. You should be getting back to the house. You're shivering."

Charon's nightgown was almost completely covered with mud, but on her sleeve was a patch of something once wet, now dried, of a suspicious brown color. Cary wondered, as she grabbed both Flora's wedgie and Charon's weak, trembling arm, whether that stain mightn't be blood. Right then, however, she didn't have time to think about it. All that mattered was to get her sick and chilled friend into her own bed. With arm planted firmly through Charon's, Cary led the trembling young woman back toward St. Anne Manor.

When she reached the bushes next to the front door, Cary dropped the remaining wedgie into their thick foliage. She intended to retrieve it later. As Cary guided Charon through the front door, Janette, who was passing down the hall, cried out. "Oh, Charon! My word, what happened?" The sickly, mud covered young woman said nothing as Cary helped her along. As she drew closer, Janette turned to Cary. "Is she ill? How did she get outside in her nightgown?" She fluttered to Charon's side. "Why, she's shivering." Janette clutched at Charon's other arm. "You just come right on to bed, young lady."

Charon didn't argue, but went with head bowed passively.

Janette helped Charon into a clean gown, letting the soiled one drop to the floor in a heap. She grimaced in distaste as she glanced quickly away from its sight. Then she led the girl to bed. There, Charon became so overwrought that she sobbed hysterically. "I can't remember! I can't remember anything. Why was I out there?"

"Perhaps you were sleepwalking, dear," said Janette

mildly. "People do, you know, and often find themselves waking up in the strangest places." Charon stared with piteously pleading eyes to Cary, as if begging her friend to agree.

"That's true," replied Cary helpfully. "Why, I knew someone who woke up on an outdoor trampoline in some stranger's back yard." Cary forced herself to remain brisk and cheerful as she improvised an outrageous tall tale. Bending down, she glanced at Janette. "I'll get rid of this for you." She tried to sound nonchalant as she gingerly lifted the stained and muddied garment from the floor.

"Would you?" Janette beamed in grateful relief as Cary transported it away from view.

Once inside the privacy of her own room, Cary stuffed the gown into a brown paper shopping bag. She wanted to find out exactly what that suspicious stain on the sleeve might be and intended to ask her young doctor to analyze it for her.

After meeting him to hand over the garment, she hurried back to St. Anne Manor. It was imperative, she felt, that no one know what she had been up to—particularly Charon. The girl was already too frightened as it was. Once in the house again, Cary decided to spend the rest of her afternoon keeping Charon company.

Chapter Twenty

"Charon, can you remember anything at all about what happened last night?" Charon's room, with the curtains drawn shut, seemed restfully dark. Only one dusty beam of sunlight filtered in through a crack of windowpane not completely covered. As its light meandered in a jagged path from floor to dressing table and from there to the foot of Charon's bed the young woman watched it wearily fade into the shadows. At Cary's question, her haggard and pale face assumed an expression of hunted weariness. "I don't know." She sighed dolefully. "I've wracked my brains—but nothing."

"Did you dream? Try to remember, Charon!"

"I—I remember that I dreamed." Charon bit her lip and frowned. "But I can't remember anything about it."

"Try!" Cary leaned forward. "After you went to bed, do you remember getting up?"

"Oh, I don't know." Charon lashed out in exasperation. "What difference does it make?"

Cary wondered if she ought to tell Charon, who didn't yet know, about the missing woman, about the blood in the kitchen and about the wedgie's mate. "Charon," she finally said with a sigh. "Flora's missing. We have reason to believe that she died by violence."

Charon gasped. A stricken look came into her eyes as she clapped a hand to her mouth. "No, it can't be! And I had one of her shoes. What happened to the other one, Cary?" She straightened and turned on her friend with blazing eyes. "I asked you, what happened?"

"We found it." Cary turned her head, unable to face her friend. "In the kitchen."

"In the kitchen." Charon spoke musingly. "What else did you find there? I have to know."

Cary was unable to bring her voice about a whisper. "Blood!"

Charon shuddered. "But you didn't find her body? She's still missing?"

"Yes."

"Then there's hope." Charon stared grimly past Cary toward the patch of wall under her dressing table. "I have to find her. I must."

Cary's eyes followed those of her friend and she started in alarm. "Charon, no! Don't go into that passageway alone. You mustn't."

Charon said nothing and Cary leaned forward. "If you want to explore in there, let me know and I'll go with you. Fair enough?"

Charon didn't reply, but instead buried her face in her hands. "Where will it all end, Cary? It's nothing short of a nightmare."

"I know." Cary stood, went over to the dressing table. Bracing herself against one end, she pushed, straining until the bulky piece of furniture slid reluctantly across the wood floor.

"What're you doing?" Charon stared in alarm.

"I'm moving this thing so that horrible exit'll be blocked. No one comes in and no one leaves." She stared significantly at her friend.

Charon's voice grew suddenly cold and she stare at Cary with the eyes of a stranger. "Sometimes I hate your guts."

Cary whirled, startled by the change in her friend. "That wasn't necessary." She glared at the pale girl. "I know you're ill, but you can still be civil. After all, you were the one who asked me down to help you."

"Why don't you just mind your own business?" Charon's voice cut with unexpected harshness.

"Listen!" cried Cary in exasperation. "Do you want me here or don't you?"

"It doesn't matter—anymore."

With a cry of anger, Cary flounced from Charon's room, slamming the door hard. Hurrying to her own, she flung open the closet and yanked out the smaller of her two suitcases. She flung it on the bed, then opened it.

Pulling out a drawer, Cary then scooped out the underwear neatly folded inside. She carried an armload over to the suitcase and threw it inside.

At that moment, however, her packing was interrupted by a knocking on her bedroom door. "Yes, what is it?" Silently hoping it was Charon apologizing after a change of heart, she waited for an answer. To her disappointment, she heard instead, the prim voice of Marie. "There's a telephone call for you," she said, then added disapprovingly, "I think it's that doctor friend of yours."

Cary's heart gave a lurch. Feeling her face grow warm, she answered eagerly. "I'll be right down." She tripped lightly down the stairs, ony a few yards behind the taciturn Marie. Once her feet hit the first floor, she half-ran toward the parlor where the telephone had been set, its receiver off the hook on the coffee table.

"Dr. Gautier?" Her voice trembled as she realized, with some surprise, that her heart was racing. A surge of warmth spread through her at the sound of his serious, reserved voice.

"Do you have an hour free? I just received partial answers to some of my inquiries."

He's so formal, thought Cary, yet she remembered that afternoon when they had been together in his car. The look in his eyes had been one of yearning. For one ecstatic moment Cary thought he had returned her own budding feelings. But he had turned away. When he had looked at her again, his manner had changed to one of courteous neutrality. "Miss Matthews, are you still there?"

Cary jolted out of her reverie. "Oh, yes. I can see you anytime."

"Under the circumstances, I think it would be tactless of me to meet you there. I suggest the same place as before."

"I'll be there as soon as I can." After hanging up the phone, Cary slipped out the front door and hurried toward the road. She knew she'd get to their meeting spot before he did, but she didn't mind waiting.

Passing around the road's end, she spotted a fallen tree on the left side. She went toward it then sat down. As she waited, the time dragged by. Glancing at her watch, Cary saw that she had been there almost fifteen minutes. With a sigh, she settled back. After twenty-five additional minutes, she uttered a stifled exclamation of annoyance and alarm, then clambered off the log to start back.

She returned just in time for dinner. It was an unpleasant affair. Marie sat stiffly, staring anxiously at a spot somewhere in the center of the table. Speaking to no one else, she absently fingered the little silver cross hanging around her neck. Cary noticed that the old woman seemed to have aged ten years since the morning. Janette, on the other hand, tried to carry on as usual. She chattered with forced cheerfulness about irrelevant subjects until Marie could stand it no longer.

". . . and so I said to him," burbled Janette, overinflecting to achieve a passably mirthful tone, "I think you raise the prices when you see me coming, Mr. Beauregard. And he said . . ."

"Shut up, Janette!" Marie's thin voice cut through her younger sister's words like a cold knife.

Janette immediately obeyed, looking ahead. Ordinarily Cary would have felt anger at such brusqueness, but tonight she was relieved, even grateful to Marie for shutting off the flow of chatter. In the ensuing silence, Cary glanced anxiously at Charon. She stared in sullen silence at her food but ate nothing. "Charon, hadn't you better eat something? Your health—"

"I'm not hungry." Something hard in her tone stopped Cary from pursuing the subject. Like Janette, she fell silent.

She ate more out of habit than appetite. Although the food, tonight a steaming jambalaya, was excellent, the day's horror had left her nauseated. Foremost in her mind was the strange non-appearance of her ally Dr. Gautier. She wondered what had happened to him. Although the sensible portion of her intellect told her that he had probably been detained on a medical emergency, the more irrational recesses screamed that he had been hurt, or that he had decided to leave her to fight the unknown battle alone.

Now that Flora had disappeared, the manor's inhabitants had to do all the work themselves. Cary helped Marie and Janette clear the dishes. At their insistence, she left them

109

to wash and dry while she wandered out to the porch. Its sofa-sized glider faced outward toward the black marsh beyond. With a gloomy sigh Cary threw herself upon it. Swinging back and forth, she stared pensively at the deepening twilight.

After a short while, Jerico came and sat beside her. "Hello, Jerico." Cary wondered what it was she might have learned about the youth had Dr. Gautier shown up.

"I missed you at dinner," he said, after a pause.

"Where were you?"

"I didn't feel like coming in from the bayou just to eat."

"You mean you were actually out in the water?" Cary turned to him curiously. "How do you get around? You can't walk out there safely."

"I have a pirogue," he replied.

"What's that?"

"It's a flat-bottomed boat especially designed for the bayou." He turned to her earnestly. "I'd like to take you riding some time. It's beautiful out there. I know you'd like it."

"Thank you, Jerico."

He stared at Cary with sad, adoring eyes. "You know, I think I'm . . ." Cary turned to watch him with carefully concealed amusement. "What I mean is, you're the nicest lady I've ever met. And you're beautiful, and . . ." Jerico bit his lip in confusion. "I—I like you very much." His words blurted out in a rush. "You're the only one who's ever been nice to me."

"Thank you, Jerico. I like you too." Cary replied non-committally just as Marie called to her from the screened front door.

"Telephone for you."

Cary jumped eagerly to her feet. "I'm coming!" She ran into the house, hurried over to the phone and lifted the receiver. "Yes?" She hoped her caller was Jed Gautier. As the voice answered, a rush of relief warmed her. "I'm so glad you called," she said. "I waited for about forty-five minutes. I hope you didn't come later."

"I'm sorry you had to wait." He replied with apologetic regret. "My car broke down." Cary detected a note of bitterness in his voice. "I tried to call you, but something was wrong with the lines I guess."

110

"I hope you can get it fixed," she replied.

"I'm working on it now. Fortunately I was able to get the parts I needed from that little gas station in Fleur-de-Lis. I ought to have it finished by tomorrow."

"What about—well, you know, what we were meeting to discuss."

"It's something best not talked about over the phone." He paused, then added grimly. "I don't like you being there in that place. I can't help feeling it's dangerous." If you only knew, thought Cary with a sardonic chuckle, but she remained silent. He continued. "As I already said, I'll find you a place to stay in Banting any time you like."

"You know I can't do that." Cary felt touched by his apparent concern. "Anyway, I'm not alone."

"That's what worries me." The young doctor's voice was calm, devoid of all inflection.

"What do you mean?" Something in his lack of tone alarmed Cary.

"Never mind for now. If you insist on staying there, at least lock your door when you go to bed tonight. Promise me."

"I promise, I promise." Cary sighed. "But I wish you'd at least let me know what you've learned."

"Tomorrow," he replied. "Even if I have to walk the fifteen miles to the manor."

"I hope *that* won't be necessary." Cary smiled quietly at his earnestness.

"Well, be careful now."

After saying goodby, Cary hung up. Passing out into the hall, she saw Jerico standing next to the door. His face had darkened into a scowl. With a thudding sensation, Cary realized that he might have been listening and was thankful she had been discreet. "Good night, Jerico," she said.

"Who were you talking to?" He asked the question curtly, almost rudely.

"A friend."

"A man?" Jerico's voice sounded strangely brittle.

"Jerico, really! I don't think that's necessarily any of your business."

"It was a man!" He replied in the type of triumph that implied he had guessed the worst and had been proven right.

111

"Yes, it was." Cary answered him in a burst of exasperation as she headed toward the stairway. "And now that you've pried that out of me, I'm going to bed."

By the time she had climbed halfway up, however, she felt embarrassed at her outburst and turned around. She saw Jerico standing at the foot of the stairs, his head hung dejectedly. "I'm sorry." She felt truly ashamed. "It's just that today has been a rough day and I'm jumpy. Please don't feel bad."

The youth nodded and turned away. "Good night," he mumbled and headed toward his own room.

"Poor kid," murmured Cary as she wandered down the hall. On her bed rested the suitcase, open as she had left it. She closed it absentmindedly and set it on the floor. She would attend to packing later—after she met Dr. Gautier, learned what he had to tell her and was able to inform him of her own decision to leave St. Anne Manor for good.

Chapter Twenty-One

After spending about an hour writing letters in bed, Cary drifted off to sleep. She sank into a strange dream. She sludged along in a chest deep mire of mud and from afar she heard Dr. Gautier calling out her name as he searched for her. Jerico floated past, rowing a curious raft-like craft.

In her dream she begged him to pull her out of the slowly deepening mud. "Jerico, help me!" She had stretched her arms to him as he drew the log boat closer.

Jerico leaned over its edge, staring at her with mournful, longing eyes. "You must promise to love me." He had waited, still staring sadly.

"Jerico, Jerico help me!" Cary's throat strained as she screamed soundlessly. "Pull me out!" She had called to him again.

"You promise to love me?" He had asked the same question a second time, not moving until she answered.

"Jerico, I'm sinking!" Tears had rolled down her cheeks as she fought the sucking sludge.

"I said, you must promise to love me first." He had remained obstinate, leaning over the edge to wait.

"I can't!" She had screamed. "Can't you understand I can't promise that?"

Jerico had not replied, but without saying goodby, had rowed away. She was left, trapped in the mire to die. In her dream, Cary began to cry. Sobs wrenched her body as she sank slowly deeper, her mind paralyzed with abject fear.

Gradually she realized the sobbing came from outside

herself. It grew louder until Cary suddenly woke with the startled awareness of something wrong. Muffled crying wafted through her walls from Charon's room.

Cary lurched out of bed and jammed her arms into the sleeves of her quilted housecoat. Tying it shut, she hurried down the unlighted hall.

She tried Charon's door. It was unlocked so she walked in. She saw the double balcony window swing open. Charon, wearing only a flimsy nightgown, crawled along the railing. When she turned and saw Cary, she thrust herself over.

"Charon!" Cary lunged for her, but it was too late. Charon dropped down and clutched the railing with both hands as she hung free.

As Cary reached to grab her wrists, Charon let go. Her weight, unsupported by anything, was more than Cary could hold. She stared in horror as Charon dropped into the bushes twelve feet below.

"Charon!" Cary whispered her name in horror, certain that she was either dead or seriously wounded.

Just then, Charon stirred, then struggled free of the bushes. She backed away and stared up at Cary. To Cary's shocked surprise, Charon bared her teeth into a triumphant smile and laughed mockingly. "I wanted to die, but you never let me. Now it's too late to stop me." Then she whirled and ran toward the inky shadows of the bayou.

"No!" Cary gasped and leaned over the railing. "Charon! Charon, come back!" But her efforts were futile. As the white-gowned figure disappeared into the darkness, Cary heard more of the same derisive laughter.

In an instinctive response, Cary followed Charon over the balcony. She hung by her hands, then let herself drop into the bushes below. Fighting her way free of their painfully prickly branches, she stumbled across the darkened lawn toward the retreating girl. Then Charon stumbled. Cary ran toward the fallen girl, lunged and caught her.

"Charon, no!" She tried to sooth her. "Whatever's wrong, we can solve it."

"Let go!" Charon struggled desperately to free herself from Cary's grip.

Cary, remembering the dead-eyed child and Jerico's words held on tightly. Tonight, anything seemed possible.

114

"Charon, they not only want to kill you, but they'll take your soul as well. They'll turn you into a zombi!" Had it been daylight, or had circumstances been different, Cary's words, once uttered, would have sounded ridiculous to her own ears. "Please come back with me."

"Leave me alone!" With surprising strength, Charon pushed Cary away. "I killed Flora and now I must die!" Cary grabbed the girl's ankle and held tight as Charon fell crashing into the grass once more.

"I mean it, Charon. I saw that child. Jerico saw him too. They turned it into a zombi!" Who was she blaming? Cary wondered even as she spoke whether she thought the three old women were responsible or some unknown evil still lurking unsuspected. She ducked Charon's swinging fist, for the girl remained hostile.

She stumbled to her feet, kicking herself free from Cary's grasp, then ran toward the dimly illuminated reeds and moss hung trees beyond.

Cary tried to follow but stumbled over her long nightgown and fell. "Ah!" gasped Cary as her chin crashed into the ground. Dizzy with pain she lay there, engulfed in despair. Why had Charon suddenly seemed so suicidal? It didn't make sense. And tonight she had acted like a wild animal, furious to fight free. As Cary labored to her feet she heard a piercing scream.

Charon's voice, crying out in horror, rent the night's silence. Running toward it, Cary dreaded what she'd find. "Charon I hear you! Where are you?" Her own voice, sounding small and inadequate, seemed to evaporate into darkness.

"I'm stuck! In quicksand!"

"Keep talking!" Cary plunged into the ever soggier ground. "I'm looking." Finally her feet sank into ankle deep mud. "Hang on, you're sounding closer." Cary struggled to find the proper direction in which to turn. Mud surrounded her. It splattered on her nightgown and caked in her hair.

"I'm so frightened." Charon's voice seemed swallowed by darkness.

"I know. So am I. But keep talking anyway. It's the only way I'll find you."

As she searched, Cary thanked God for the dim illumination from the moon. It reflected upon the ooze in which she struggled, making it glitter. Ahead, Cary saw surreal shapes that great gnarled roots formed as they emerged from their bed of mud. Low branches and moss caught at her as she flailed past. From afar, Cary heard the sound of hissing, and somewhere ahead came a splash.

"Oh, my God!" Suddenly, as she remembered the alligators in the bayou, a sudden terror gripped her. Had that splash been caused by one of those giant flesh eating reptiles? Had her nightmare been a premonition?

"Cary, I'm sinking!" Charon's shrill, panic stricken voice cut through Cary's own private fears.

Something glided past her in the mud, but Cary hardly noticed as she pushed her way through another low hanging veil of moss. Suddenly she saw a faint outline of a thrashing figure. It fought, trying to escape from a waist deep morass.

"Don't panic! I see you." Cary hurried toward her. She pulled off her bathrobe as she came within reach. Clutching one end, she flung the other to Charon. "Grab onto it!" She heard her own voice grow shrill and urgent. "Grab tight and I'll pull you out."

Charon obeyed, moaning hoarsely as Cary braced herself as best as possible behind a tree. Pulling with all her strength, she felt a slight yielding. "It's working. Hang on!"

"I am." Charon gasped. "Keep pulling."

Cary felt the weight at the other end tug loose. Gradually the strain on her arms lessened as Charon stumbled out of the quicksand onto a somewhat more solid foundation.

"I thought I was dead for sure!" Charon's hoarse breathing sounded loud as she stumbled toward Cary. "I wanted to die, but I never realized it'd be quite so horrifying." The young woman shuddered.

Cary supported her trembling friend as both started toward the direction they remembered having come. "Thank you." Charon whispered as she collapsed onto Cary's shoulder. "And about today. I don't know what came over me, but I'm sorry."

"It's all right," replied Cary brusquely. After the ordeal she had just gone through, she didn't feel like talking. Furthermore, despite Charon's apology she still felt hurt at the treatment she had received throughout the day. "I feel

116

as if I've just come to my senses in a way," Charon stumbled forward, her face pinched. "It was almost compulsive. Actually, now that I think back, it *was* a compulsion the way I behaved, and it was one I don't understand. It came upon me suddenly."

"Yes, it did," replied Cary grimly. Then she softened. "I'll try to understand, but sometimes it's hard."

"I know." Charon sighed then glanced around. "Cary, where are we?"

"What do you mean?"

"This isn't the way I came!" Her voice sounded in sudden alarm. "I know it isn't. Do you suppose we're lost?"

"No—no, we can't be," replied Cary uncertainly. "We weren't that far into the swamp to begin with."

"Are you sure?" Charon stifled a sob as she twisted her neck to peer through the surrounding canopy of foliage. The mud water seemed deeper as the two young women stumbled on. "What'll we do?"

Cary, in response, turned her charge gently in the opposite direction. "It's getting deeper now. We'll go back the way we came. We're bound to find our way out sooner or later."

"Or sink into a bog of quicksand or be eaten alive." Charon sounded so dangerously close to the edge of breakdown that Cary suppressed the urge to remind the girl that being there was her own doing.

"No, we won't," was all she said. She tried to speak in the soothing manner of a nurse in order to hide her own growing terror, but Charon burst into convulsive sobbing anyway. Her crying became shriller and louder until suddenly she began to scream.

"No! Charon don't!" Cary grabbed the girl's frail shoulders and shook her. But her screaming continued. In desperation, Cary raised a hand to slap her. Slamming first against Charon's right cheek with the back of her hand and then the left, she managed to quell the rising rush of hysteria. The distrait young woman made a hiccuping sound then fell silent. Cary grabbed her arms firmly and dragged her toward shallower water.

The two of them stumbled and fought their way forward until the swamp mud started deepening again. "Now what're we going to do?" Charon sounded forlorn and weak.

"I don't know." Cary lost all her old forced boyancy as the grim reality of their situation truly settled upon her. "I don't have any more answers."

"Please forgive me?" Charon asked meekly. "I didn't mean for anything to happen to you, and if it comes down to it, save yourself at my expense if necessary."

"You once helped me when I needed it badly, and I can't forget your kindness to me then," replied Cary staunchly. "I'm not leaving without you!"

"All I ever did was give a little money to help you finish school. I never risked my life for you, and it's just not fair to let you do that for me." Charon's voice trembled as she reached the verge of tears. Suddenly she stiffened. "What's that?" Cary followed the direction of the girl's eyes, then cried out in hopeful surprise. Playing against the gnarled trunk of a tree was a light. Its beam was lower and more concentrated than the moon's pale rays or any other natural source. It flitted from trunk to trunk.

"Someone's out there!" Cary's heart pounded in exultant hope.

"Maybe we should call to them." Charon trembled suddenly.

They yelled until their voices grew hoarse as they pleaded in unison for assistance. In reply, they heard the splash of an oar followed by a cry from Jerico. "Keep talking!" A vigorously working oar paddled toward them.

Suddenly Cary noticed an elongated form about ten yards away. Though partially submerged, its massive head showed above the water's surface and caught the moon's pale rays on its wet, glittering hide. Behind its eyes and elongated jaws, the body floated under the surface and appeared to be nothing more than a shadow blending into obscurity with the bayou's darkness.

She stared into its eyes, so small and dark, became numb as the creature glided silently toward them. "Oh Jerico, hurry up!" Cary's words trembled as she failed to control the fear-tightened muscles of her throat.

Just then his light finally played upon their faces. "Oh Jerico, there's something in here with us!" Cary sounded barely audible to her own ears.

He glided the pirogue masterfully to them. "Of course there is," he replied in cold scorn. "It's their home, this swamp, and they have every right to live here and catch what they can to eat. It'd serve you right too, because it was a stupid thing for you to do." He reached down to help Cary hoist Charon on board as the giant reptile slithered closer. He reached to pull Cary onto the boat. The craft nearly capsized as she lurched chest first over the side. When she was safely on board, the young man turned to her. "You could've been buried alive in all this damn mud." All three stared in horrified fascination as the huge alligator paddled by. It disappeared with a slash into deeper water.

"It's all my fault." Charon averted her eyes in shame. "She was only—"

Her words were interrupted by Jerico's mockingly satirical laugh. "Out biting necks again, Charon my sweet?"

Immediately the girl stiffened and turned her face away. Cary turned angrily to the youth. "Why did you have to go and say that?"

Jerico shrugged. "Maybe because it's true." He murmured more to himself than to Cary. "After all," he said, forcing a jocular tone, "she's descended from a long line of goblins, ghouls and vampires."

"You're not the least bit funny." Cary spoke with grimly controlled anger through clenched teeth. "Can't you see how upset she is?"

Jerico gazed steadily at Cary then turned back to his business of manning the oar. "Sorry." His apology was polite but insincere.

After an uncomfortable silence, Cary leaned forward. "How did you know we were out here?"

"You two harpies weren't exactly quiet, you know. I'm a light sleeper. Anyway, that bush you both chose to land in happens to be right outside my bedroom window."

"I'm thankful we woke you." Cary smiled gratefully.

"Yeah, sure." He turned his back on both young women.

Upon reaching nearly solid land, Jerico sprang from the pirogue and tied it to a tree. After helping Charon out, he guided her from the grove. Cary followed. Standing at the edge where lawn met swamp glowered Marie. Janette stood wringing her hands anxiously.

"Are you all right, Miss Charon?" When Janette saw the

the girl being supported by Jerico, she rushed forward with open arms. "I'll help you, poor child. Oh, Jerico, it's a blessing you found her!" Her dark eyes flashed beyond to Cary. "Yes indeed, I'm thankful you even saw her."

Cooing, she took the shivering girl from Jerico and started to guide her toward the house. After a few yards, Charon straightened and pulled away. "Thanks, but I can walk by myself." She trudged on unsteady feet up the path to the darkened mansion. Cary lagged behind, feeling utterly spent.

As she stood the young woman felt a creeping sensation tingle down her back. The sudden awareness that she was being watched burst upon her. She whirled, then clasped her hand over her mouth. A tall thin spectre stood motionless with back to the moon. "Oh my God!" she mumbled. As the figure inched closer, she was gradually able to discern Marie's features from the shadows. "Oh!" Cary sighed in relief. "You gave me a scare."

Suddenly, however, Cary's fear returned in greater intensity than before. The gaunt but familiar face had tightened into a mask of hatred as Marie's cold, black eyes glared balefully at her.

"You were warned to get out of here!" Marie's upper lip contracted into a snarl. "This idiocy you two staged tonight —it was your doing. She hadn't ever run off like that before you came. Go back where you belong! Go anywhere, but I'm warning you, lady, get out of here!"

Marie's lips parted to reveal gleaming white teeth. They gave her hate-filled face the appearance of an untamed carnivore. "I haven't the power to force you to leave, but if you stay, I won't be responsible for what happens to you!"

When Marie edged yet closer, Cary became filled with desperate, overpowering fear for the woman semed to have turned into a malevolent animal. As she screamed, then whirled to flee from the remorseless woman, mirthless laughter followed her from behind. With head reeling, Cary stumbled across the soggy lawn. She pushed into the house. Her heart thudded as she careened upstairs to the safety of her room. After turning on the overhead light, she slammed the door. Its lock had a key, which she

120

turned. After it clicked into place, Cary walked to her bed on trembling legs.

After a few minutes of relative comfort, lying collapsed on her bed in a room illuminated by the sensible bright glow of electricity, Cary began to feel silly about her fear. She began to wonder how she could ever have gotten so shaken over Marie. The eeriness was caused less by the old woman's rudeness, she decided, than by their eldritch surroundings. Or was it? The uneasiness returned to Cary as she remembered that contorted, hate-filled face. Marie's words had been a distinct threat. Hearing the low murmur of Janette's voice, however, Cary went to Charon's room to help.

The old woman was helping the girl change from her mud-soaked gown into a dry, clean one. As Cary walked in, Janette smiled gratefully. "I'm so glad you're here. Will you take over for me please?" She spoke apologetically. "I guess I'm getting old but I'm so tired after all the excitement."

"You go on to bed, Janette." Cary grabbed a towel and turned to help Charon dry her hair. Janette murmured thanks and hurried out.

"Everybody will be better off when I'm dead." Charon's eyes stared hollowly at the floor.

"Nonsense!" Cary helped the girl to her bed.

"It's true. I've caused so much trouble."

"Charon, what was the real reason you ran away tonight?"

"I already told you, I wanted to die—" She turned away.

"Then why were you so panic-stricken when you were caught in the quicksand? If you were running into the swamp to die, it should've fit right in with your plans."

A painful silence ensued. Finally Charon broke the silence. "I–I wanted to find Flora. I don't know why I thought she'd be in the bayou, but that's what I felt." The sickly, pale girl lapsed into a morose and impenetrable silence.

"I'll make you some hot tea." Cary spoke briskly to break the gloom. "We both need it." In reply, Charon nodded.

After about fifteen minutes in the kitchen, Cary returned with a steaming pot and two sturdy mugs. She poured the

121

greenish brown liquid into both, then handed one to her friend. "Drink this."

Charon held the mug between trembling hands. "Thank you for coming down. No matter how I change or how horrible I become to you, please believe that I appreciate it."

Cary shrugged. "It wasn't that I sacrificed a rich life full of fun and fortune or anything. If I was able to help at all, I'm glad, but at the time I considered your letter of invitation an escape."

Charon laughed mirthlessly. "Escape! Look what you've escaped into—a house ful of hostility, a friend who's disintegrating and a swamp full of deadly peril."

"I'd still rather be here with you than in that miserable insurance office in Cleveland," replied Cary staunchly.

Charon smiled. "Thank you." She paused, then finally broke her own silence. "I've made a will—"

"Oh, Charon, why be so morbid?"

"I'm not morbid, I'm being realistic. As of this week I own the place. I've lived up to the terms of the will and everything is mine. As a landowner and person of modest wealth, it's only sensible that I should make a will."

"Well, if that's your reasoning, then I guess you're being sensible.

Charon shrugged. Although she said nothing, the expression in her eyes betrayed her turbulent inner feelings. "When I die," she said, "I'm leaving everything to you. You're the only person I trust."

"Charon!" Cary felt more exasperated than anything. "You're young. Now that you've been here the required five years you can leave. Why don't you go someplace where the climate and surroundings are healthier. When you get out of here, you'll probably outlive *me!*"

Charon smiled sadly. "I've left generous bequests to Janette and Marie, of course, and I've even placed funds in trust for Jerico's education. Even though he's horrible I feel a certain responsibility toward him. You get everything else."

"Charon!" Cary felt embarrassed. "Please don't talk like that. You won't die for years and even though I appreciate the thought, you probably have relatives who should inherit."

122

"I have no one," replied the girl. "I am the last known descendant of Louis Parveau. The *last!* If I don't bear children the family will die out—as well it should."

Cary shivered. "Charon, you frighten me."

Chapter Twenty-Two

Despite the night's excitement, Cary woke early. Though she was physically exhausted, she felt tense and edgy. She dressed and headed downstairs for breakfast.

To her intense dismay, Marie was ascending and would pass her half way down the winding flight. After last night's unpleasantness, Cary would have preferred avoiding Marie altogether. She wondered if her greeting would be met by stony silence or a curt insult. To her surprise, however, Marie spoke with painfully strained courtesy. "I hope you slept well, once you found your way to bed." The old woman's voice was icily polite. With a tight smile on her lips, she gazed steadily at Cary from cold, hard eyes. Cary replied in kind.

"Very well, thank you. I hope you too had a satisfactory rest."

"Most satisfactory. And now, if you will excuse me, I shall retire to finish some chores." With those cryptic words, Marie had swept past her to the second floor. Cary stared after her departing form, then hurried downward. As she reached the bottom step, the phone began to ring. Hurrying to answer it, she heard Dr. Gautier's voice.

"Oh, I'm so glad you called!" Cary felt a glowing rush of warmth.

"What happened?" The young doctor had caught the underlying tenseness in Cary's words.

"I—I can't talk about it here." She glanced around, anxious that no one should overhear.

"I'll meet you at the usual place." After saying a quick goodby, he hung up.

Cary peered out the window at the bleak sky. It looked cold out, so she hurried to her room for a sweater. Quietly closing the heavy front door she hurried down the path leading to the road. The wet chill that had descended upon the bayou pierced even the heavy knit of Cary's Irish cardigan and caused her to shiver. As she hurried to the road's curve, however, the chill faded. She grew almost warm, for in a distance Cary saw Dr. Gautier's car. She broke into a run as he drove to her. Lurching to a stop, he threw open the front right door. "What is it?" His face grew tight as he turned to her. "But you're all right, aren't you?"

But as Cary started to explain what had happened the previous night, he stopped her. "Before you continue, can you come with me? Just as I was about to leave I received word that I'm needed." As Cary nodded, he made a U turn and headed back in the direction of Fleur-de-Lis. "It's just beyond the village," he said. "A premature birth."

As he sped along the bumpy road, his face set in an intent frown, Cary related what had happened the previous night. After finishing, she turned to him. "Well, that's it. What do you think?"

The young doctor shook his head. "The more I find out, the less I like. It all fits in."

"What do you mean?"

"We'll start with the nightgown. I analyzed the stain and found what I hoped I wouldn't." He sighed. "The brown spot was blood. Human blood."

"No!" Cary stared at him in horror.

"But that's not all. I wanted to see you in order to tell you what I learned from that little book you lent me—you know, the *Lycaon*."

"What about it?" Cary fought to contain her dread.

"I spent a few evenings last week translating it, and it's very strange. The book is all about lycanthrophy—a phenomenon sometimes known as vampirism."

"You mean like Wolfman or Dracula?" Cary snorted in mirthful scorn.

"It's a far subtler version of all those old cinematized

125

myths. The *Lycaon* describes a condition far less theatrical but none the less evil."

"You don't believe in all that, do you?" Cary stared at him, mildly shocked at his apparent superstition. "You, a doctor of all people, should be free of such nonsense."

He rebuked her gently. "I'm not saying that vampirism exists in any kind of supernatural form—I don't believe in it myself. As a doctor, however, I'm well aware that the human mind is our greatest mystery. Take ESP, for example. Only a few years ago, scientists scoffed at its mere mention. Today reputable testing laboratories in many developed nations are seriously studying it. They're getting results too. About ten years ago the Boston Police Department risked ridicule by hiring a well-known mentalist to help them solve the strangler killings. He was able to describe correctly happenings and events that only the police, the victims and the killer himself could have known about. Or what about the way vengeful medicine men in primitive societies are able to kill through mere suggestion? Miss Matthews, these things, however fantastic, have all been documented. Some we're just beginning to understand. The others, well—" The young doctor shrugged.

"But what does it all have to do with a poor sick girl who imagines herself to be a—a werewolf?"

"Unexplained phenomena do exist. Unless something is an out-and-out lie, there exists at its core at least a grain of truth, and in that lies its natural explanation. For instance, do you know how the Dracula legend got started?" He stared at Cary challengingly, then continued. "In the Balkan wilds lived a nobleman known as Vlad the Impaler. He was named for his method of executing enemies and prisoners of war. He would impale them alive on huge stakes and leave them to die."

Cary shuddered. "How awful!"

"You see though, don't you, the suggestion there of piercing the body, of blood? Only a few generations transformed the wooden stakes into teeth. Even then those stakes survived as the method by which a vampire can be killied. Humans at one time practiced cannibalism. Even today, the Leopard Men of Africa can hypnotize themselves into believing that their bodies have been turned into the animal spirits that are supposed to have possessed them. As a medical man, I know that violent cravings can and do exist. Just because a hunger for the taste of blood is a medical or psychological rarity doesn't mean it hasn't happened or that it can't."

"Like seeing only one white crow proves that white crows exist." Cary stared gloomily through the front window as the car speeded forward. A tide of nausea thickened in her stomach. "And you think that Charon is one of those—medical rarities?"

"I can't form an opinion based on what little I know of her. I want to remind you that you've received threats against your life. What happened last night proves, in my opinion, that she's become dangerous to herself at least and possibly to you. Nothing supernatural about any of that."

"Okay, you've made your point." Cary agreed reluctantly. "But I'm not leaving now. Yesterday I felt differently, but Marie made me angry. No one's going to scare me out of a place."

"You've got courage." He regarded her with veiled admiration.

Cary smiled. "My mother used to say I was pigheaded."

"Well, that too." He shrugged and Cary laughed.

"What about Jerico?"

"I don't know yet, but what little I've heard sounds bad. I called at his last school and the principal refused to give me any details. Instead, he went into a hushed, disapproving tone of voice and announced, rather pompously, that he merely pitied the boy's family."

Cary scowled. "Then we'll never know."

"We might. I've got an old friend in Baton Rouge who's making discreet inquiries."

"I'm almost afraid of what we'll learn. He's been so ghoulish lately." Cary's mind wandered back to his comments of the night before.

"He saved you though. Perhaps it was only because he knew the others had been awakened, but still it's a point in his favor. He could've left you to die."

Dr. Gautier had driven through the main street of Fleur-de-Lis and out the other side. Gradually the density of trailers and houses thinned, dwindling into scattered shacks. He stopped at one isolated habitat located about

127

five miles past the village outskirts. "Well, here we are," he said, "you might as well come in. I may need your help."

Cary meekly complied. "You know I've never done anything even remotely related to medicine, don't you?"

He turned to smile at her as he pulled a large satchel from the back seat of his car. "Don't worry, I won't ask you to do anything beyond your capabilities." Suddenly they both heard the shrill scream of a woman in pain. Dr. Gautier shoved a smaller bag into Cary's hand. "Here, take this." Leaving her standing with the case in her hand, he ran toward the front door just as it was opened from inside by a man.

Cary surmised from the anxious manner in which he stared at both of them that he must be the woman's husband or father. "I'm so glad you come, Doctor." He grabbed the young physician's arm. "Bella's in here. She's bleedin' real bad." Both men disappeared inside as Cary followed over the threshold. "The baby's come too soon!" There was no mistaking the fear in the man's voice.

"Miss Matthews, boil some water!" Dr. Gautier's voice rang forth clear and commanding. Cary glanced around for a kitchen but saw only a wood-burning stove set in one corner. Three cast-iron kettles of varying sizes lay piled beside it. As she began clumsily to load wood into the stove's front opening the woman's husband hurried to her aid. "Here, I'll do that. Pump's out back. You get the water." He grabbed the middle-sized kettle and shoved it into Cary's hand.

Hurrying out the door, the young woman lugged the heavy container by its wire handle. Behind the house stood a rusty hand pump. After setting the kettle under its spigot, she grabbed the handle and pumped.

It creaked shrilly but for seemingly endless number of downward thrusts, Cary worked but received no results. Gradually she felt pressure build up from within. After about ten more thrusts, rusty water spurted erratically into the kettle. When she had filled it, the young woman lugged it back to the house.

If Cary thought the kettle had weighed a lot when it was empty, she now had ample reason to know just how heavy it could become when filled. As she clutched at the handle its weight cut into her palms. The heavy water-filled kettle

128

banged against her shins, causing her to flinch in pain. She knew she'd have yet another collection of bruises tomorrow. The woman's husband ran out the front door as she entered, grabbed it from her and set it on top of the stove.

"Maybe we ought to heat smaller amounts at one time," she suggested. "That way we'll have hot water sooner than we would if we wait for this whole big thing to boil."

"Good idea!" The man lifted the pot off the stove, reached for a two-quart pan hanging from an overhead beam and dipped it into the water. This smaller container he set on the stove to boil. From the other room, the woman's moans grew louder, more intense.

As they waited for the water to heat, the man anxiously paced the floor. His lips moved in what Cary guessed was silent prayer. Though his swarthy face, deeply lined, gave evidence of the hard, primitive life he led, his black eyes shone clear. His big calloused hands were clenched inside the pockets of his shabby trousers. Every so often he'd glance at the still placid water and utter an ejaculation in French that Cary suspected was a curse. She wanted to console him, to assure him that the water only *seemed* to be taking forever to boil, but knew he wouldn't appreciate her intrusion into his private thoughts. Just then, Dr. Gautier burst from the back room, his shirtsleeves rolled to his elbows.

"How's the water coming?"

"It's almost ready," she replied. "We had to pump it first."

He strode over to the pan and gazed into it. Little bubbles were gathering around the sides and bottom. "Good," he said. "Bring it in to me when it reaches a full boil and then start some more immediately."

When Cary brought the pan to his side, the young doctor was gently instructing the woman in French on the way to push the child forward during her labor contractions. Cary, who had studied that language with more success than she had Latin, found herself barely able to understand the dialect he used. "Have you put more on to boil?" As he stared at her with burning eyes, he seemed to be a totally different man.

"Her husband's doing it right now," replied Cary meekly.

"Good! Now get a rag, wet it, wring it out and bring it

129

back to me. Use one of the sterile cloths from my small bag." Cary obeyed. "Let her suck on it," he said, continuing. "She's thirsty but I can't let her drink any liquid. She might throw up and choke." The woman grabbed the cloth from Cary's hand and pressed it to her parched lips.

"Find out if there's any sugar or honey in the house. If so, soak another rag in a saturated solution of sugar water or honey. If she were in a hospital right now, she'd be getting a glucose solution intravenously. She's not, however, so we'll have to make do with what we have." Cary hurried to obey once more. Out of the corner of her eye she saw Dr. Gautier's big hands gently stroking the woman's matted hair from her face.

"Here, hold this in your mouth," he said as Cary handed her the sticky, honey-soaked cloth. "It'll give you energy." As the woman went into another contraction, however, she groaned, her face contorted in pain.

"Can't you give her something?" Cary stared helplessly at the agonized woman.

"I could, but some of it'd get into the baby and slow its own reflexes. As it is, a premature child has difficulty surviving. If doped, its chances will diminish to nothing and I'd rather not take the chance."

The hours passed. The woman's climaxing screams finally merged into one long, bloodcurdling shriek that seemed to last forever, and her husband prayed aloud as he crossed himself. Then all was silent; and both Cary and he heard a loud slap followed by the angry squalling of an infant. When the young doctor called her name, Cary rushed to see what he wanted. To her surprise, he stepped into the doorway and handed her an incredibly tiny little creature wrapped in a ragged wool blanket. "See that its father keeps it close to the fire. Warmth and lots of it is the only way it'll survive." As she took it in her arms, he added, "Your job is to wash it. Use some of the boiled water, but make sure it's cooled to a comfortably warm temperature."

"How's my Bella?" The woman's husband lunged anxiously toward the young physician. "Is she all right?"

"You must keep her very quiet and warm. See that she's fed soft food—especially milk and eggs—and hope for the best. I gave her an injection to slow the hemorrhaging."

"Jack—?" The woman called faintly from the now darkened room behind Dr. Gautier.

"Bella!" The distraught man ran to join his wife.

When Cary had almost finished sponging the newborn infant clean, she looked up. To her surprise her friend stood watching her. "Good work." He smiled at her approvingly. His face was streaked, his own dark hair matted, and blood covered his once white shirt. The look of satisfaction on his face, however, was unmistakable.

Cary smiled. "You saved her."

"I think luck. God and my meager medical skill saved both of them." Cary suddenly understood why he needed to remain here with these poor backwoods people. In this place his skills were really needed by people who otherwise had no one to help them. She suddenly felt the need to tell him of her feelings.

"Dr. Gautier, remember when I first met you, I asked why you'd ever stay here when you could practice in the city and be wealthy? Well, I think I understand now." He smiled and his pleasure was unmistakable. Just then, they heard a knocking at the door.

He admitted a rotund, gray-haired old woman. "I heard Bella went into labor," she said. "I saw your car. Can I help?"

He regarded the old woman seriously, and evidently decided she was competent. "Can you stay a few days? Bella's not able to take care of the baby—not just yet. She can nurse it, and should, but everything else—" He shrugged.

"I understand." Her expression was intelligent and knowing as he repeated his instructions to her. "I'll look in on them both tomorrow," he said, as they started out the door.

Both he and Cary entered the car in silence. Neither spoke as he drove her back toward St. Anne Manor. "Will they have missed you?" he finally asked.

"It's none of their business, really," she replied. "Anyway, everyone there seems too wrapped up in his own miseries to care about anyone else."

"I want to thank you," he said. "You were a big help."

Cary shrugged. After another silence, his car pulled up almost to the manor's driveway. He turned to her. "Please call me if anything out of the ordinary happens. No matter how small, it may mean something or portend danger."

As he gazed, almost longingly into her eyes, she felt like reaching out and touching his hand, but because Cary's ego still rankled from her recent rejection she held back. Looking into his eyes, however, she could almost convince herself that he really cared about her. Was it possible that she was more than merely a woman in danger that his ingrained sense of chivalry felt obliged to help? Cary fervently hoped so.

It was only in his eyes that she saw signs of the natural man hidden behind his oddly formal façade. Even there, however, Cary didn't know how to interpret what she read. He was different from any man she ever knew. Aloud she said, "That's very kind of you, Dr. Gautier, to put yourself out for me this way. I'm becoming a dreadful nuisance." Cary shook her head wearily. "But I'm so tired of it all. I don't want to talk about it anymore."

"As you wish." The young doctor glanced at her quizzically. "What would you prefer?" He laughed, almost sadly. "Or is this your way of telling me you want to get out of the car and leave?"

"Oh, no!" Cary replied almost too hastily, then stopped in mild embarrassment. "That is, unless you've got better things to do and secretly want me to get out of your hair." She forced a nervous chuckle, for she really wanted to remain in the security of his presence indefinitely. "Anyway, you're probably exhausted."

He turned to her. "No, it's not that, Miss Matthews. Please believe me—you're not in my hair at all!"

Cary whirled the ring on her right middle finger. "You know," she said, "after all we've been through together it seems as if we could call one another by our first names—that is, if you have no objections. You may call me 'Cary' if you want."

The young doctor smiled. "I've been waiting for that. The way I was raised it wasn't considered polite to address a lady by her given name until she gave you permission. I know that's old-fashioned and horribly rigid, but people tend to be bound by what they were taught early in life." Cary remembered the informality of her own college days and wondered about the effects of such stiffly formal cour-

132

tesy on his social life. She asked him about it. "I tried to change when I was in school," he replied, "but could never feel comfortable about breaking the old codes. It's silly, really. I'm as programmed as an experimental rat or one of Pavlov's drooling dogs. You may call me 'Jed', of course, if you wish."

Cary, who had always sensed the strength and hidden fire behind his stiffly formal manner, found that she had grown to care deeply for this painfully reserved young man. "How did you like school?" She wanted to keep him talking, to remain there beside him in his battered car.

He stared grimly through the front window. "Intellectually interesting," he replied finally.

"That's a rather cryptic answer." Cary spoke softly, but with growing understanding.

"That's about all there was to it." Jed averted his eyes. "Beyond intellectual stimulation there was nothing. Except third floor walk-ups, part time jobs and endless meals of starch. Fortunately that kind of life is bearable, and even pleasurably adventurous when you're young and have something to look forward to as I did. I don't regret any of it."

An almost awkward silence fell upon both Jed and Cary as they stared through his front window at the starless sky. "I think there's going to be a storm," he said, finally.

"I hope not, but I'm afraid you're right." Cary sighed as she reached for the door handle. "I guess I'd better be getting back."

"Don't forget—if anything happens, call me immediately. The whole business is turning nasty and I don't like it. And of course, if I hear anything I'll call you right away."

"I promise." Cary smiled warmly. "And thanks." She hurried up the drive to the waiting mansion.

133

Chapter Twenty-Three

That evening as Janette prepared supper alone, occasional, distant claps of thunder punctuated her activity. Cary offered to help, but in vain. The old woman insisted that it was her duty and struggled on with the job that had been Flora's. She did let Cary set the table, but as she set down the fifth plate, Janette stopped her. "You needn't bother setting a place for Jerico. He said he wasn't eating dinner."

"Not eating dinner?" Cary frowned. "At his age—"

"I don't claim to understand that boy." Janette almost snapped at her. "He's my own flesh and blood—grandchild of my mother's only son and yet I don't know what goes on in his head. Why, the way he talks and the way he runs off to hide in that boat of his. I just don't know."

Cary felt a surge of pity. She had never seen this side of the old lady before. Janette seemed soft and completely devoid of all passion—even outdoors when she danced around the fire her ecstasy seemed docile. Yet Janette was a woman, with all the fears and anxieties women feel. Cary never really realized it before. "It's his age." She tried to speak soothingly, to comfort Janette. All the while, however, she hoped that her own doubts about Jerico didn't show in her voice. "Teenage boys are always a little hard to live with, I've heard. They're rebellious. Unfortunately some of them get into trouble, but they usually grow out of it. I'm sure that's why Jerico acts the way he does."

"We're the wrong ones to handle him." Janette shook

her head in defeat. "A boy like that needs a father—a man who can keep him in line. Or an understanding mother."

"His own parents?" asked Cary delicately.

"They died." She replied grimly. "His father Jack was killed by an inept doctor—a quack some say, who took all his money, promised a cure, then left him to die. Anna, the boy's mother, soon after died of grief."

"And that's why Marie hates doctors." Cary was beginning to understand.

"Marie loved Jack as if he had been her own son. When he died, it soured her on all doctors. As far as she's concerned they're all full of empty promises, lies and greed. You understand, don't you, that's why she's so unreasonable about your friend. It's poisoned her mind. She feels all doctors care about is money."

"Not all of them," mused Cary, half to herself, but Janette didn't hear.

"It frightens me the way that boy's growing up—all strange and spooky. He screams at his elders, then goes running off to be alone in the swamp." Janette sighed in resignation. "Oh, well, it can't be helped, I guess."

She handed the girl a steaming plate of baked vegetables. Clutching two hotpads, Cary took it from the old woman then set it in the center of the table beside a platter of pork chops. "Another thing you could do for me is to summon Charon," said Janette. "She's well enough to eat down here tonight."

Cary found Charon in her room, surprisingly dressed in a rose taffeta floor-length gown. Its full skirt, decorated at the hem with ruffles, was supported by a hoop petticoat. The tight bodice, ornate with rows of fine but yellowed lace, ended in a 'V' at her waist. Long full sleeves puffed off her shoulders. These had been gathered with ribbon at the elbows, then allowed to billow freely below. Rich rose cloth, trimmed with more of the same fine lace, rippled over her slender wrists. The dress's low scooped neckline gave Charon's bare shoulders and pale face a curiously cameolike appearance. That effect was heightened by the old-fashioned, long curls into which Charon had twisted her blond hair. As Cary walked in, she found her friend standing in front of the mirror, gazing admiringly at herself. "Charon!" When she heard Cary's surprised voice, she whirled, smiling in slight embarrassment.

"I found these in an old trunk," she said. Cary noted with surprise that her usual faint drawl now seemed exaggerated. "I decided to amuse myself by trying them on. They fit very well, don't they?" She pirouetted slowly, arms held away from her body. She looked like an antique mechanical wind-up doll—one with white porcelain face and lovely costume. "I even found a fan." She lifted an ivory fan from her dressing table and fluttered it coquettishly.

With growing unease, Cary realized that the costume strangely suited Charon, as if the young woman had belonged to an earlier, long dead era but had been misplaced in time. Trying not to let her own increasingly morbid imagination run away with her, Cary spoke with hearty cheerfulness. "You look lovely, and the curls really fit nicely with the costume. I'm afraid it's going to be a little awkward at dinner though, which is the reason I came upstairs."

"Oh, yes, dinner." Charon pursed her lips disdainfully but didn't argue. As she glided toward the bedroom door, her skirts swayed gently from side to side.

Once downstairs, she slipped into her chair and waited. "My word, that's a lovely dress, Charon. Where did you ever find it?" Janette smiled in polite surprise.

"In a trunk in my room. I put it on and found it comfortable."

To Cary, it seemed as if Charon's choice of the word 'comfortable' had acquired sinister levels of meaning. Certainly she couldn't be referring to physical comfort. To fit into one of those dresses, a woman had to lace herself tightly inside a corset. No, it seemed rather as if Charon's mind was already lost to the present as she traveled backwards into time. Cary said nothing, however, because there wasn't anything she could have said. She ate in apprehensive silence, listening as Marie's crisp voice cut through her thoughts.

"Such a pretty gown, of course, but impractical. I really hope, Charon, that you don't accidentally drip any meat juice on it. I'd be sorry to see you ruin it."

"I'm not a child," replied the young woman haughtily. "I don't intend to eat sloppily. You know I never do."

Just then, Jerico burst in from outside. They all heard his footsteps crashing toward the dining room. They whirled in their seats as he stopped short at the door. All four waited uneasily as the youth gasped breathlessly to catch his wind. "What is it, Jerico?" Marie turned to him. "There's still food enough if you care to join us."

He didn't reply, but stared at Cary. His mental state seemed to verge on panic. "I have to talk to you—*alone*. It's important!"

Seeing the veiled fear, horror in his eyes, Cary rose from her seat.

"Now you let Miss Cary finish her dinner, d'ya hear?" Marie frowned at her grandnephew as she rebuked him.

"No, that's all right. I'll be right back." Cary replied rapidly then walked past their table toward the youth. With her eyes, she questioned him.

"Outside." Into that one word Jerico packed all the urgency of his mission. When he had closed the front door behind them both, Cary turned to him.

"Now what exactly—"

He grabbed her elbow and steered her toward the trees that grew beyond the house's west end. "Out here. I found her."

"Found who—?" Suddenly the sickening realization of whom he meant filtered into Cary's brain. "Flora?" She asked in dread, knowing the answer.

"She's dead. Horribly mangled. I found her in the reeds."

"Didn't you look there before?"

"Yes. That's the horrible part of it," he replied. "I already checked those reeds once, and she wasn't in them. Somebody put her there since this morning."

Tingling with dread, Cary half ran by Jerico's side. When she saw the remains, she let out a stifled scream then gagged. The woman had been dead for only a few days, but that was enough to change her appearance. Even beyond the horror of decay, however, was the body's mangled condition. Sensing her unasked question, Jerico replied. "That could've been caused by wild animals." She heard doubt in his voice.

"Was it?" Cary too found it difficult to believe that

137

animals could have inflicted so much damage on poor old Flora. What shocked Cary most, however, was the expression of horrified fear on the face. "It's awful!" She shuddered.

"I didn't know what to do when I found it." Jerico spoke apologetically. "Everyone else in that house is half-off their rockers. You're the only one with any sense. I don't know what you can do about it, but somebody has to know."

From behind them a horrified scream pierced the velvet night silence. Both whirled. In their excitement and horror, they had failed to notice the front door open. Neither had heard the feet, encased in rose taffeta slippers, glide stealthily across the soggy lawn behind them. Yet there stood Charon, a pale, horrified girl cringing from the gruesome sight as she clasped the back of her hand to her mouth. "What—what have I done?" Her voice trembled as her eyes fixed glassily upon the dead woman. After interminable breathless seconds, a sigh escaped from her lips and she crumpled to the damp grass in a deep faint.

"Help me carry her back to the house." Cary struggled to keep the panic out of her voice. "We'll worry about Flora later." Together they transported the unconscious girl toward St. Anne Manor.

"My Lord, what happened?" Janette stared pop-eyed at the two. Panting and struggling, they hoisted Charon's dead weight up the front steps and across the threshold.

"She's had a terrible shock." Cary gasped in reply. "You'd better get some brandy or whatever you have."

After depositing the unconscious girl on her bed, Cary turned her over to loosen the tight dress bodice. "Thanks, Jerico," she said. "Would you cover Flora with a tarpaulin, please. After I undress Charon and put her to bed, I'll phone Dr. Gautier. He'll know how to call in the police." With a nod, the boy walked from Charon's room just as Janette hurried in. She clutched a bottle of corn mash liquor.

"It isn't brandy," she said apologetically, "but it was all we have in the house. I think it's Flora's."

"It'll do." Cary's shaking fingers fumbled with the complex back clasp of her friend's antique gown. Janette set the bottle and shotglass down and joined her.

"I'll help," she said. "But hadn't you better call your doctor friend?"

"Yes. If you can finish getting her undressed by yourself I'll go down and do it right now."

"Go ahead. I'm more familiar with these clothes than you." Janette deftly finished the back and slipped Charon's arms out of the billowing sleeves.

Cary turned on a light in the deserted parlor as she hurried to the phone. As she picked up the receiver, however, Marie stepped through the open doorway. "I see you're trying to call your friend the doctor." She spoke with the same scornful tone she used whenever mentioning the word 'doctor'.

"Yes, I am. Charon's sick and probably in shock from what she saw out there and it's something I'm afraid we can't handle by ourselves."

"Quite the contrary," replied Marie coldly. "Remedies exist that are many times more effective than those handed out by quack doctors. Charon can be cured by those."

"Wild herbs and voodoo spells?" Cary didn't bother to hide the sarcasm as she picked up the receiver. A flicker of anger burned in Marie's eyes, but Cary no longer cared. She dialed, then waited for an answer.

She heard nothing, however. The silence was broken by neither dial tone nor busy signal. Not even so much as a muted hum came through the receiver.

"I took the liberty of disconnecting the phone." Marie spoke smugly, in grim triumph.

"Well, you can just go and reconnect it!" Cary snapped back as she slammed the receiver down angrily.

Marie folded her arms obstinately. "I think not. I've had just about enough of your barging in here and trying to change our lives. That phone stays the way it is. I'll cure Charon my own way." She glared with cold anger at Cary, who stared back with growing horror.

"You're mad!" she whispered, unable to take her eyes off the old woman. "Don't you realize that shock can kill a person?"

"So can bad medicine, but nobody thinks about that."

"Just because fifteen years ago a doctor couldn't save your brother's son is no reason to blame all doctors."

"They killed him on purpose. They made him promises,

139

took his money then left him to die." The memory of his death, and her anger, must have festered in Marie's memory like a swollen tick. "The finest lad who ever lived and they killed him, the quacks. The money grubbing quacks!"

As she swept out the parlor door, Cary called after her, but to no avail. She stared in consternation at the dead telephone, then slammed down the receiver with an angry curse.

Chapter Twenty-Four

Cary stared after Marie in outraged silence. Biting her lips to hold back a scream of rage, the young woman muttered a word she saved for especially trying situations like this one. Her head pounded. After passing several seconds waiting for her tumultous thoughts to calm, Cary yearned to take action.

She ran to the hall closet. Inside hung the thin coat she had brought down in the mistaken assumption that Louisiana weather was too mild to need anything heavier. Since she intended walking to Fleur-de-Lis, using the public phone and calling Jed, Cary knew she'd need it. Outside the night had grown bitterly cold.

A clap of thunder, seemingly right over the roof, set all the window panes rattling. Fluorescent brightness flashed against the night's black sky but Cary paid no heed. She flung open the closet door, yanked out her coat, and threw it over her shoulders. Running to the front door, she pulled it angrily open onto weather that weighted her with dismay. The rain fell so heavily that it hid the path and road beyond from view. The wind, blowing into the house, sharpened those thick droplets into hard pellets that lashed cruelly against her cheeks.

"Planning to leave us?" Marie's mocking voice startled Cary from behind. She whirled to gaze into her adversary's smug, triumphant face. "According to the radio," continued Marie, "this is the start of a hurricane. Are you really sure you want to be out in it?"

Cary's indrawn breath hissed against her clenched teeth.

"You're quite pleased with yourself, aren't you Marie? If that girl upstairs gets worse, it'll be your fault."

"It'll be God's will." Marie's black eyes glittered. They seemed to have become inhuman orbs in the impassive yellow mask of her face.

"You're the one!" An overwhelming urge to confront Marie with everything swept over Cary. "I know you practice voodoo, but I guess you don't believe in it enough. When you thought the magic failed to scare me or kill me, you began laying boobie traps—like that upstairs carpet and the gas you turned on after locking my door and windows. You should have stuck to your voodoo because murder's illegal."

Marie's eyes widened at the attack. At first their expression seemed startled. Almost immediately they hardened into a cynical gleam. "Think what you like, you absurd little minx." Her lips curled into a sneer. As she whirled to climb the stairs her soft chuckling shrilled into loud laughter.

Cary chilled, suddenly afraid. She felt isolated, cut off from her only contact with outside and safety and he had no way of knowing. "Oh, dear God, help me!" She whispered in horror. Gripped by a sudden spasm of fear, Cary ran upstairs to lock herself in her room.

She kept the light on. She, slumped in her chair, shivered. She stared forward, her eyes burning. For what she waited, she didn't really know. The hands of her bedstand clock moved with agonizing slowness as one hour passed followed by another. Outside, the storm burst and raged above. She listened as raindrops beat noisily against her windows. A flash of lightning streaked across the sky to blaze trees and shrubs alike with color searing brightness.

And yet another five, ten, twenty minutes passed while Cary waited. The wild pounding in her ears had long settled into a steady throb of which she seemed abnormally aware. "It's all anxiety," she said, pondering that physical fact. "People under stress usually have heightened awareness of their own bodily processes." Her knowledge, however, didn't make the feeling go away. The throbbing continued, along with the faint, high frequency hum of blood coursing throughout her body.

She glanced at her clock for the hundredth time or more

and saw that it was only midnight. Cary sighed. "Another six hours to go." She yearned for dawn more than she had ever wanted anything in her life.

Suddenly, a deafening clap of thunder exploded overhead. The house shook violently and a pane of glass, propelled by the bellowing wind outside, exploded from her bedroom window. Jagged shards whirled across the room to crash onto her floor and rug. Cary bolted from bed in alarm.

Then the electricity failed. It left her in darkness. "Oh no!" Urgent fear washed over Cary. With shaking hands, she groped for her flashlight. She stumbled to her desk where she remembered putting it. She pulled her top drawer open, reached inside and found nothing. Another clap of thunder roared, followed by lightning. During the brief flash, Cary glanced rapidly around the room as her eyes searched for the missing light. She saw only the familiar surfaces, covered with her own paints, pencils, stationery and clutter. "Oh no!" The flashlight was nowhere in sight. Although she cried out, her quick mind already worked desperately for a solution.

"Candles!" Cary felt exultant at having found an alternative source of light. She remembered seeing some in the bedstand drawer when she had first moved in. Groping her way to it, Cary yanked it open. As she reached inside, her palms and fingers touched a row of candles. Grabbing one, she reached again to search for matches. She found none there, but remembered the pack in her purse.

After interminable rummaging, Cary found them. She pulled out the matchcase and struck one with trembling fingers. With its flame she lit the candle, then shielded the tiny fire by standing between it and the wind gusting through her broken window.

A far off peal of thunder rolled. Another sounded directly overhead. A second tinkling of glass from somewhere above heralded another broken window. Cary whirled to check further damage as more lightning lit the landscape. She gasped in horror. In the exploding brightness she saw a dim and shadowy figure moving about her room. It merged almost immediately into an expanse of what Cary had always thought was bare wall and disappeared.

As she lunged after it, another gust of wind crossed into

143

the room. Her candle, its flame already flickering wildly, blew out entirely. Cary cried aloud in exasperation then kneeled to relight it. She held the match flame against its still hot wick until its wax saturated tip ignited. She stood once more, guarding the flame with her cupped left hand.

Staring at the spot through which the figure seemed to have disappeared, Cary groped at the wall for any protrusion that might betray an opening. Obviously this was yet another entrance into the secret network of passages behind St. Anne Manor's walls. As she searched, Cary found nothing. Finally, with exasperation, she pushed a shoulder against its smooth surface. To her astonishment the wall yielded. A three foot wide expanse sank backward at a slight incline. Still shielding the candle with her free hand, she shoved a second time.

Another burst of thunder and lightning both rattled and illuminated the room as Cary burst through her opening into the black labyrinth behind. She glanced around, saw nothing, then started forward. Frightened and angry by the sinister games some unknown person was playing with her, Cary decided to confront the situation once and for all. "I know you're here somewhere!" Her voice echoed strange but weirdly steady to her fear sharpened ears.

She advanced, step after step, treading cautiously. The candle beamed strongly in her hand. "I want to say," she called out, "that I'm sick and tired of your clumsy attempts to scare me away. And when I didn't frighten so easily you tried to kill me. By planting traps you almost succeeded too, but now we're alone together." Cary marched relentlessly forward. "I'll find who you are once and for all!"

Somewhere in the blackness beyond Cary's candle she heard a creaking floor. She lurched forward in search of the unknown someone. The difficult corridor was complicated, however, by the pitch darkness that surrounded her meager light. Yet Cary had an iron determination to find out, even if it meant her death, who was trying to kill her.

Her heart clutched in horror as a deathly white visage appeared, then disappeared up ahead. The dry yellowed skin that sank into its facial contours reminded Cary of the pickled flesh of a mummy. Two beaming eyes burned from its pallor and the wrinkle mouth had been painted bright red. Long white hair frizzed past the creature's waist.

It lifted one clawlike hand and gestured for Cary to follow.

Suddenly, fingers from behind reached from the blackness and clutched her wrist. Cary screamed and struggled against an unknown adversary's superior strength, but to no avail. She felt herself suddenly shoved toward the left with violent force. As she plummeted into space, Cary screamed again. Her voice shrilled against the inky blackness.

As she crashed, shoulder first against a stone floor below, Cary cried in pain. Rolling onto her back, she lay doubled over and groaning while waves of blinding agony washed over her. She fought for breath and consciousness.

Gradually the throbbing in her shoulder and chest lost its original intensity, until she was able to think rationally once more. Her first concern was to find out the sort of prison she had been caught in and to escape from it. After moving her arm gingerly to see how badly she had been hurt, Cary groped in darkness around the pit wall until she felt the higher surface above. Escape would be especially difficult now that her candle was gone, but she'd have to succeed somehow.

By straining, jumping and forcing herself to ignore the pain in her shoulder, Cary managed to chin herself up and out of the pit. As she did, she saw an arc of light about eight yards beyond, widen then disappear. Evidently she was near a room, an entrance back into the house itself. Cary stumbled to her feet and groped down the now dark passage.

She pushed her shoulder against the spot where the figure had disappeared. Nothing yielded however. She moved to the right and repeated her action, then to the left. On her fourth try, the unyielding solidarity gave way. Heartened by success, Cary pushed again. A bright crack appeared, then widened. She pushed herself through to inside.

To her surprise, the room was the same one she and Charon had discovered together. She stepped into it and glanced around more thoroughly than before. She hadn't had the chance to really notice the fireplace before. It was huge, and built of rough antique bricks that covered one wall. Hanging above it, Cary spotted a portrait she hadn't seen before. Its subject was an ethereal young woman. She wore the same rich, rose taffeta gown that Charon had found and long blond curls. One tiny gloved hand clutched a hard looking leather riding crop. Behind, the artist had depicted the entrance to St. Anne Manor. Underneath the painting and inscribed on brass had been fastened a placard that identified the painting's subject as Sophie Parveau. Cary stared in fascination at the face of a woman who would later be murdered by her husband.

Suddenly the storm killed St. Anne Manor's electricity for the second time. But the darkness did not descend soon enough for Cary to miss the startling resemblance of Sophie's portrait to Charon. The face, hair and attitude were as identical as if Charon had posed in place of her ancestor. Only in the eyes did Cary detect a difference, for the artist had captured a hard cruelty in Sophie's that seemed entirely absent from Charon's.

Cary stood in the darkness, absorbed in thought connecting past to present. Memories of days at St. Anne Manor crowded into her mind. She relived the horrible evening when she had found the mutilated cockerel and its companion threat in her bed. Her mind wandered back to the night she had lost her footing on the loosened stair carpet. Her vision of the scene seemed so clear that Cary relived it. The way as she lay sprawled on the bannister, Charon had run to turn on the hall light. She remembered Marie, running to Charon's side from her room on the far right of the hall. After a short interval, Janette had joined her half sister—trudging out-of-breath from the left.

Cary's memory flow halted abruptly. Why had Janette come from the left when her room was next to Marie's on the opposite side of the spiral staircase? Only Cary's and Charon's were located to the left of it—that and the door opening from the kitchen stairway.

Suddenly icy horror clutched at Cary as she realized the implications of her discovery. It had been Janette who had sneaked up the backstairs after untacking that carpet? Always Janette seemed to discover Charon after one of the girl's nightmares, and Janette had been the first inside Cary's room after the attempted gassing. Janette!

Suddenly, a soft chuckling behind made Cary whirl. In the darkness she saw no one. "A portrait of Sophie Parveau, mother of Lucie. She was a woman said to be as cruel and depraved as her husband." Just as Cary recog-

146

nized the gentle drawl, altered by a hitherto unfamiliar intensity, a match flickered to light a candle. Janette beamed a ghastly smile at Cary. Although her cheeks still dimpled sweetly and her expression was apologetically meek, her eyes betrayed her benign exterior. In them gleamed an exultant hatred that could only have been born of madness.

Cary gasped. "You!" She still found Janette's guilt hard to believe. "Of all the others!"

"Fooled you, didn't I?" Janette chuckled. The sound, with its intensity magnified by the surrounding darkness, seemed particularly horrible. The light, flickering across her face, gave the old woman's countenance a satanic glow.

"Why?" Cary's head numbed.

"Why? Why? Why, indeed!" Janette answered irritably a question she evidently considered insulting. "Because I've been a servant all my life. A servant when I should have been mistress of St. Anne Manor."

"What are you talking about?"

"Do you think old Louis became celebate after Sophie died? Do you think a man with his lusts and appetites could ever relinquish the companionship of women? Just because he never married again, because no man of his own class would allow Louis to take his daughter, doesn't mean there were not others."

"What are you saying?" Cary, overcome by fright and tiredness, felt suddenly stupid.

"I'm saying that there was a woman with whom Louis lived after Sophie's death. A woman to whom Louis gave a child." Janette stepped closer to glare into Cary's eyes. "I was that child. I am the natural daughter of Louis Parveau. Brought to this house as a child with Marie and her brother—treated like a servant even though I was mistress. Papa knew who I was, and what I was, but the world refused to recognize my lineage. Well, no more, do you hear? After I'm rid of Charon this place will be mine—as it rightfully always has been!"

Janette's voice changed to a ghastly conversational tone. "At first, I tried to kill her, but then you came down so my plan had to change—to one much cleverer, I think. I determined to drive that girl to suicide. I almost succeeded too,

147

but you got in the way and stopped her. With you gone, it should be easy."

She stepped still closer. "But first I have to get rid of you." Janette smiled apologetically. "Oh, I don't want to do this, but you wouldn't leave. Marie suspected, I think, because she warned you. But to no avail. Don't you understand? It's nothing personal." Her hands extended into claws as she reached for Cary's throat. Cary stepped back, out of reach.

"I want to know something first." Cary stared into Janette's eyes, forcing herself to hide the sickening fear that churned inside her. Janette had pushed her into that pit with the surprising strength of madness. Cary knew she was no match for the old woman. She knew her only hope, however slim, lay in keeping Janette talking. "Is Charon really a loup-garou, or did you plan that too?"

Janette smiled. "Very clever of me, wasn't it? Being at the right place at the right time—making sure the blood was smeared on her face. Comforting her when she awakened, then helping her wash so that no one would know. She's so very suggestible."

Janette began to enjoy bragging. "Overhearing you talk about that superstitious fool of a gas station boy gave me a particularly brilliant inspiration. He was so easy to lure and kill, and I knew you'd both think only the two of you had known of your encounter with him. Of his warning to you, I let you all draw the obvious conclusion," Janette's dimples deepened. "Of course, papa was indeed a loup-garou—a real one. Such a problem it became when he roamed. I'm sure city doctors have a fancy Latin name for it nowadays, but when I was a girl, we knew what such people were really called. Yes, it was so easy to lead her on once I found my source for blood."

"For blood?" Cary felt faint.

"I heard Jerico laughing about how you ran away from the mausoleum—frightened because of a noise you thought you heard. Well, what you and Jerico don't know is that a whole passle of brats is in that building—turned into zombis from a weed that grows wild in the swamp. I milk 'em for blood—like cows. Of course, you'll never live to tell."

Janette's once soft laughter shrilled into a maniacal
148

shrieking. "And poor old Flora—always snooping into my things, that one was. When she found my birth certificate though, I couldn't let her live. She would've told Marie, who never knew I was only her half sister. After all," Janette shrugged, "Mama would never have talked about those things. Worse, she might've told Charon. She liked Charon." Cary felt numb beyond horror as Janette came with claws outstretched toward her neck. As Cary's own hands reached forward to struggle, lightning flashed through the hidden room's high, narrow window. It illuminated yet another figure slipping through the secret passage.

Charon, dressed again in Sophie's faded gown, glared at Janette with baleful eyes. Her skirts rustled. They seemed to whisper soft curses as she glided toward the suddenly terrified old woman. In her upraised hand, Charon clutched a glittering knife. "You did it to me!" she whispered, her face contorted with hatred. "You tried to make me believe that I was a loathsome creature of blood and death. You tried to convince me that I was the loup-garou who went around tearing out the throats of children!" Charon's free hand reached to grab the trembling old woman's shoulder. "You wanted me to kill myself but you failed." Another clap of thunder drowned out Janette's reply, but Cary saw the old woman's eyes light with terror.

Suddenly a third figure emerged from the secret passage —a tall, gaunt creature of indeterminate age and gender. Cary recognized in it the same one who had lured her into the catacomb that night. Janette saw too, and gasped. "Lucie!" Her words trembled with concentrated terror.

Charon stared too at the thing, then whispered, "Grand-mother?"

Lucie whirled, freezing all of them with the stare of her piercing blue eyes. When she spoke, in quaint but educated French, her voice crackled shrilly. "You!" She pointed a gnarled finger at Janette. "You tried to destroy the child of my only baby." She stared tenderly at Charon. "So like your mother, but so much more beautiful. I pray to God you've been spared our horror." Resting her eyes on Cary, the ancient hag—Charon's only living ancestor—advanced. "I tried to make you understand the danger. You alone had the power to save her." She whirled again to Janette who

149

cringed. "But your sin was most horrible, and for it you must die!"

Cary stared with a fascination that numbed her senses. Although vaguely aware of a thumping noise from beyond the room, she paid no attention. As Lucie lunged, Janette screamed and the pounding grew louder.

Suddenly the locked door burst open. Through its splintering wood crashed Jed, shoulder first. Just as he landed in a sprawl on the floor, Cary stared paralyzed as Janette cried in panic, lunged away and scrambled through the broken attic window. The creature who was once Lucie followed close behind. Through that window far off in the distance, Cary saw dim lights moving toward St. Anne Manor. Then, overcome by horror, Cary melted into a dead faint.

Chapter Twenty-Five

As Cary fought free of her swoon, Jed's soft voice drawled beyond her hearing. Her brain struggled to regain consciousness. His voice became clearer until she realized he was actually kneeling beside her. Keeping her eyes closed a little longer than she had to, Cary listened to the words he believed he was speaking to an unconscious woman. "I should have done the manly thing and taken you into Banting whether you wanted to go or not. I should never have brought you back here. If you're hurt, I'll never forgive myself!" He bent and gently kissed her on the forehead. Cary thrilled as his lips pressed against her skin. "I love you," he whispered. "If anything had happened to you—"

Cary suddenly felt awkward and a little deceitful, but what he said gave her such an indescribable sense of joy that she wanted to hear more. However, the knowledge that Jed thought he was talking to someone unconscious made Cary feel like a common eavesdropper. "Even when you go away," he continued, "I'd be happy just knowing you're alive—not killed because of my negligence. Oh Cary!" Jed stroked her face, then clasped her limp hand in his own. "I know you'll leave. Why shouldn't you go and find someone worthy of you? I wish it could be me, but I know better. I could never be what you want in a man."

Cary knew that now was the time to wake up. "How do you know what I want in a man? Are you a mind reader?" She spoke with half humorous acerbity, then opened her

151

eyes. Jed fell silent in embarrassed confusion. "Actually, you're exactly what I want," she added. Cary smiled tenderly as her hand reached to clasp his tightly.

"Didn't your mother ever teach you not to eavesdrop?" Jed's face softened into a longing, but disbelieving smile. Cary felt suddenly sure of herself and the strength of her own reinforcing love for him. "That's beside the point. Deceit was the only way I could ever have wrung it out of you. Anyway, I meant what I said." His hand tightened around hers involuntarily.

"You—you mean you really want to stay here in the Bayou—with me?" He stammered as she reached to him.

"Oh, yes, Jed, for as long as I've known you!"

He bent to embrace her in joy and love when a scream sounded shrilly in the night. Another flash of lightning illuminated the garret chamber and Cary saw that she and Jed were alone. A second scream sounded.

"I'm coming with you!" She stumbled to unsteady feet.

"Are you strong enough?"

"Yes." Cary started for the window but Jed caught her. "Not that way. It can be done but it's too risky." As he grabbed her arm, she glanced outside and saw the mysterious lights grow closer. Before she could speak however Jed had propelled her out the broken door and down the stairs. They reached the ground floor. As both stumbled outside, another bolt of lightning illuminated two distant figures struggling at the swamp's edge. Beyond them, the unearthly scream sounded for yet a third time.

As Jed and Cary drew closer, fighting against the shrieking wind that shoved them backward with elemental strength, they stared fascinated at Janette and Charon. Both women clasped one another in deadly struggle. Suddenly the younger one's lips contorted in an angry scream as she sank her knife into the old woman's back. The two lovers shuddered, for as blood spurted out of Janette's wound, Charon's triumphant laughter pierced even the storm's raging din.

Both Cary and Jed railed in even greater horror at the scene following. It was one that, because they were so far away, they were helpless to prevent. After Janette crumpled to the ground, Charon bent over her, pulled the knife out and turned her stomach up. Lifting the old woman's head, the strangely entranced young woman pressed her weapon's tip against her victim's throat. Sinking the blade deep, she pressed her lips into the gushing fountain of blood and drank.

"No!" Cary cried out in utter horror. Overcome, her knees turned too weak to support any weight and she collapsed. Charon, attracted by the sound, glanced up then stared back at Janette. A stricken expression of dismay spread over her once lovely, now blood dripping face. The girl, still clutching the weapon in her hand, stumbled to her feet and recoiled.

Jed lunged for her, as if he instinctively knew she might stab herself. Charon sensed his intention, however, and stepped aside as he burst past. As he fell sprawled in the soaking grass, she sank its twice fatal blade into her own chest and pierced her heart. Cary stumbled to her side as the girl collapsed.

"I had to do it," she gasped. Her hands clutched the heart wound from which gushed her own life's blood. "All these months, I felt the desire grow in me. I fought it. I tried to deny it to myself, but the craving grew stronger. And all the time—*she* thought she was deluding me into believing that I was something I had already become!" Charon laughed weakly. "Thank you for trying, Cary. I guess I knew all along that I was more scared of myself than anything else." She rolled her head toward the dead woman sprawled beside her on the grass and stared. "She tried to make me think I killed all those people, but I didn't. At least I can die knowing I haven't hurt anyone but *her*. Take care of the place." She choked, then fell very still.

"I think she's dead," said Cary.

Jed kneeled and clutched the girl's wrist in his fingers. "No pulse." He let the limp hand drop.

"So much for Charon and Janette." Cary stared ahead grimly.

Suddenly eerie lights and shadows played over the soggy puddled lawn. Both Cary and Jed looked up to see twenty shabby men marching in formation toward St. Anne Manor. Each carried a burning torch. As they saw the two dead women, Jed and Cary they slowed pace. The young woman stared, fascinated by their almost uniform

153

expression of grim determination. Jed hurried toward them, leaving Cary behind. She stumbled to her feet and followed.

"What's going on?" He ran up to the man who seemed to be leader.

"Stay outta this, Dr. Jed!" He was a swarthy man of about fifty. His black hair had grayed and deep lines cut into the flesh around his mouth. Although his clothes were shabby, he stood proudly.

"What're you going to do?" Jed stared apprehensively at their torches.

"Destroy the evil once and for all." Their leader glared at the darkened old house. "That place breeds evil. That house homes the loup-garou and we aim to get rid of it."

"The loup-garou is dead!" Jed stared intensely into the eyes of each man and repeated himself. "I said, the loup-garou is dead, killed by that girl over there lying in the grass. There will be no more killing!"

"What about my Tina?" A man's anguished voice cried out from their ranks.

"And my Jeremy?"

The leader gazed sadly at the young doctor. "I'm sorry, boy, but our killed children gotta be avenged even if the beast is dead. No one can bring 'em back."

Cary gasped, suddenly remembering Janette's words once more. "The mausoleum." She ran to the leader and clutched his arm. "The woman who did it—your loup-garou—said the children were alive in the mausoleum. Shouldn't we get them out?" Jed stared at her in surprise. "When did she tell you that?"

"Upstairs in the attic room, right before she was going to kill me."

The villager stared at her suspiciously. "Where's the mausoleum?"

"I'll take you to it. Follow me." She ran toward it and Jed caught up to hurry by her side.

"Are you sure?" he asked.

"Unless Janette was lying, which I doubt."

"In that case I only hope we're not too late. If we get there and those children are dead or absent, we'll have real trouble." Jed shook his head grimly. "Those villagers are in an ugly mood."

"For everybody's sake, I hope they're in there, alive and reasonably healthy."

Ahead, in the firelit darkness loomed the gleaming sepulchre. At night, it seemed even more forbidding than it had to Cary during daylight. She ran to its door and yanked at the padlock. "How're we going to get in?" Cary wailed in despairing frustration.

One of the villagers, however, had the answer. He stepped forward, away from the others and stalked toward the locked and chained iron granite door. He clutched an axe in his hand. Its blade glittered in the flame light as he raised it high to send it crashing against the gate. The fastening broke from the force of his blow, then clattered to his feet. The villagers cheered, but he yanked open the heavy doors and paid no attention. Jed, Cary and the others followed close behind.

"Oh my God!" The whispered awe in Jed's voice frightened Cary even before she caught glimpse of the cause. When she did, however, she too cringed in pity and revulsion, for imprisoned within the dank mausoleum were the lost children of Fleur-de-Lis. They slumped, pallid and emaciated but blessedly alive. All were surprisingly free of binding shackles, but they stared at their rescuers with the same soulless dead eyes Cary had seen once before. With a shock, she recognized among the children that strangely possessed boy she had encountered wandering alone in the swamp that horrible night.

"Doc, what's wrong with 'em? Why are they actin' so strange?" A grizzled man standing beside stared bewildered at the impassive children, but Jed had already kneeled before a dark haired little girl. Pulling a penlight from his pocket, the young doctor shined its tiny beam into her empty brown eyes. "Just as I thought." He turned to the leader. "Their passive manner and her dilated pupils suggest that they've all been drugged."

"Will they get well?" A man who had now kneeled anxiously beside the little girl stared fearfully at Jed. "Tina seems so strange."

"There's been blood loss and exposure, but they're all alive, thank God. The drug will wear off soon enough, but the memory—" Jed shrugged. "We have to get them to a hospital." He turned again to the leader. "There's a phone in the house. Go and call the State Police while I begin—"

"Jed no—the phone's still dead!" Cary clutched his arm. "Remember? Marie disconnected it."

"Oh damn!" Jed slapped an open hand against his forehead in frustration. "Somebody has to notify the state police and get them to send ambulances!"

"My truck's down the road." The leader replied with heavy forcefulness. "I'll drive into Banting an' summon 'em."

As he hurried out, Jed turned to Cary. "Go into the house and bring me as many blankets as you can—at least six, but more if you can get them quickly. Have Marie help you. She'll cooperate now." Jed knelt beside the first child to perform emergency first aid, and ignored everybody but the sick children.

Finally ambulances summoned from Banting lined up in front of the house, sharing space with three State Patrol cars. Stretchers carried the drugged children to the vehicles. The vigilante brigade of desperate fathers went with them to the hospital. After the police finished their questioning, Cary and Jed were left alone once more.

Suddenly they heard the slosh of feet running across the mud. Both whirled, their nerves still frayed from the horror. They saw Jerico. "What happened?" He gasped, out of breath.

"A lot," replied Jed. "Where were you?"

"I heard screaming, like someone in trouble. I was still awake so I ran outside. I saw what I thought was the loup-garou struggling out in the marsh. I ran to pull it out, figuring there'd be a reward if I could capture it, but when I got close I saw it was just an old woman."

"Lucie!" cried Cary, turning to Jed.

Jerico grimaced. "I don't know who it was, but I couldn't save her. The sand sucked her down too quickly."

"So much for Lucie," said Jed. "Perhaps everything worked out for the best all the way around."

"Oh, Jed. Even Charon?"

"You remember her comment about the growing craving?" The young doctor turned to her. "A mental affliction like that is hard, if not impossible to cure. She'd probably have spent the rest of her life in a mental hospital."

"You mean she became a loup-garou like her great-grandfather?" Janette's words in the garret room returned to Cary's mind.

"What about Charon's great-grandfather?" Jed stared earnestly. "Cary, what do you know?"

"Only what Janette told me about his really being a loup-garou."

Jed inhaled sharply. "So it *was* inherited. What else did she say?" Cary took a deep breath and related all the events that had taken place between her and Janette in the garret. "Even with the taint diluted by union with an outsider, it passed on to Louis' offspring. Janette had inherited his madness, although not his craving for blood."

"But poor Charon never had a chance?" Cary stared gloomily at the overflowing marsh.

"She inherited the sickness in its full strength."

Cary sighed. "I did no good by coming here."

"In a way you did. You gave her friendship in her time of greatest need and thereby comforted her. Anyway, *I'm* glad you came." Jed wrapped his arm around her. She returned the glance of love she saw in his eyes, then smiled with happiness. Jerico cleared his throat. Staring at the lovers with a pained expression on his face, he decided to be noble about the depressing way things had turned out for him. "Well, I think I'll be running along," he said, "and get some sleep or something." With a final nod, the youth turned and hurried away.

"Poor Jerico," murmured Cary. "Did you ever find out about him?"

"Tonight. Right after I heard about Lucie still being around. That's why I tried to call you. When your line was dead, I knew something was wrong so I hurried over. I hit the front door just as you started to scream. Marie let me in."

"That's surprising!"

"She was scared. Things had gotten out of hand and she didn't know what to do. She had long suspected Janette was half mad, but thought she could handle her. That's why Marie wanted you to leave, Cary. She was afraid for you but pride and loyalty to her half sister prevented her from seeking the help she really needed. She led me to the room and then fled in fear."

"Serves her right for cutting off the phone. But really,

157

what about Lucie? You mentioned her and now I'm curious."

"Oh that!" Jed shook his head. "Remember how I told you that Lucie had died? Well, it wasn't that way at all. While he was still alive, Louis managed to marry off Lucie to a nice, unsuspecting young fellow in New Orleans. She was only fifteen, but they did things younger in those days. Heredity tells though, and soon after she had given birth to her first and only child, Charon's mother, Lucie went stark raving mad."

"Did she inherit her father's craving for blood?"

"Apparently not. Possibly it's one of those taints that skip generations at a time, striking at random, but then I don't really know. About twenty years ago, however, Lucie escaped the institution where she had been confined, and I guess some instinct guided her back to the ancestral home.

"Where she lived in hiding within the manor's secret passages and hidden rooms. How lonely! She was the one who left me the *Lycaon*, you know. She knew what was happening to her granddaughter and tried to warn me."

"In her last hours, I think she became lucid. It sometimes happens that way. I hope she died believing her granddaughter had been saved."

"So do I!"

Jed gathered Cary in his arms. "But the past is dead, so let's try to forget about things we can't change."

As Jed's lips pressed hungrily into hers, Cary clung to him with both arms. The rushing surge of joy that swept away all the accumulated horror of the weeks past, left in its wake a feeling of cleanliness and rebirth.

Epilogue

Cary glanced around the parlor of the house that was now hers. "Jed, I invited Marie to stay on here."

"What did she say?"

"She says she's always wanted to travel but was never able to because of Jerico and Janette."

Jed shrugged. "She was left a generous enough bequest. If she wants to travel, then she should."

"She doesn't know what to do about Jerico."

"Jerico should be in school—preferably one that understands the minor eccentricities of a rebellious adolescent genius."

"What?" Cary stared in amazement.

"According to tests he's taken, Jerico had an I.Q. of 165. He was expelled from his last school not because he went around biting his classmates' necks or practiced Satanism but because his headmaster, a gentleman with absolutely no understanding of angry young boys, found a whole packet of what he considered 'subversive literature' under Jerico's bed. Actually, it was the kind of run-of-the-mill political garbage that many boys that age flirt around with. All he needs is guidance."

"Oh, is that all!"

"It was enough to get him expelled, but schools exist that not only can handle boys like Jerico, but even welcome them. I can make the arrangements if Marie wants. The provisions of Charon's will state that the interest on funds left in trust for him should be used for his education. That was a pretty efficient little document considering the shaky condition of her mind."

Cary didn't reply at first. "You know, I wondered what I'd ever do with the place," she finally said, "but now I know." Jed raised his brows questioningly. "This parlor, for instance, would make an excellent waiting and reception room. The others would do very nicely for patient examination. I'll help you run your clinic, of course, because it would be the kind of meaningful work I'd enjoy. I'm pretty good at accounting, you know."

"I can't let you give your house away." Jed hurried to Cary and clasped his hand around hers.

"You don't think I can *live* in a place like this, do you?" Cary glanced around, then grimaced. "I'd go nuts! Anyway, it'll be *our* place after we're married. Since St. Anne Manor sort of plopped into my lap, it seems a shame that you should have to refuse that Health, Education, and Welfare grant you just got from Washington just because you haven't any place to open a decent clinic."

"How did you know about that?" Jed stared at her in shocked amazement.

"Your mother and I had a long talk yesterday while you were out checking on that mother and baby. It was most enlightening."

"Mother's been reading my mail again." Jed chuckled wryly. "But it just doesn't seem right somehow, to take the place over like that."

"It doesn't seem right to me that those poor people should be denied decent medical treatment just because there's no place for them to get it. Anyway, as I said, the manor was more or less a gift. It wasn't as if I earned it."

"I think you're wrong about that." Jed gathered her into his arms. "These past few weeks haven't exactly been pleasant or safe for you. If you ask me, they've been downright perilous."

Cary laughed. "Okay, okay, but if that's the case, then we both earned St. Anne Manor." And Cary stifled any further discussion by kissing him.

160